MW00625621

NOME-O
SEEKS
JULIET

An Odds-Are-Good Standalone Romance

For McKenzie,
With gratitude
and affection —

Katy
Regnery
xo

New York Times Bestselling Author

KATY REGNERY

Please visit my website at **www.katyregnery.com**
Cover Designer: Marianne Nowicki
Developmental Edit: Tessa Shapcott
Formatting: CookieLynn Publishing Services

First Edition: November 2019
Nome-o Seeks Juliet: a novel / by Katy Regnery—1st ed.
ISBN: 978-1-944810-55-9

For Henry, who loves dogs as much as I do.
I love you forever.

And for Dagmar,
because she is the best of the best.

CHAPTER ONE

Juliet

NOME-O SEEKS JULIET
MUST LIKE DOGS
Musher.
Fit. Single. 34.
Retired military, honorably discharged.
I'm looking for a woman to race with me.
Training available.

"*Nome-o Seeks Juliet*," I read aloud, rolling my eyes at Silvia. "That is the *height* of corny."

"I think it's kind of cute," she says in her always-too-loud voice. "Besides, it's your name, Juliet! It's like he addressed to *you*."

"Um. No. He addressed it to a potential sled dog racing partner."

"And…?"

"I have never raced," I say.

"He says that training is available! He's exactly what you need. You have to answer this! Aren't you even *intrigued*?"

He is definitely not what I need, and my roommate is officially bonkers.

"No. Not really," I say, pushing the magazine off my desk and onto hers to make room for my laptop.

Silvia DiLeo, my classmate at the University of Minnesota, has been subscribing to *The Odds Are Good* for years. She has this bizarre dream that after we graduate from veterinary school, she'll meet a hot Alaskan via personal ad, open a veterinary practice in the frigid north, and live happily ever after.

Now I'm not one to shit on someone else's dream, but the only part of that dream we have in common is the graduating-from-veterinary-school bit…at which point I will return home to Montana and join my dad's veterinary practice, and she can try her luck at hunting down a hot Alaskan.

"I'm not looking for love, Sil."

"Neither is he!" she says. "This ad isn't in the personals section. It's in classifieds."

"Still…it's in *The Odds Are Good*," I say dismissively. "The major function of that magazine is for Alaskan men to meet lonely hearts. Ugh. No."

"Your *name* is printed." She holds up a finger. "*He's* a musher." Finger number two joins the first. "And *training* is available," she says, pushing all three fingers in my face. She nods her head with conviction. "It's a sign."

"It's not a sign. It's a personal—"

"Classified!"

"—ad."

"Are you being purposely obtuse?"

"Are you being purposely annoying?"

"Juliet!" she says, exasperated with me. "Don't you still want the fellowship?"

"Thanks for pouring salt in the wound," I say, giving her a look. "As you know, that ship has sailed."

Or will *sail*, I think, as soon as I send an email to the Doc Staunton Fellowship Board, informing them that my plans for their grant have fallen through and I am no longer able to accept the money.

"Only because the musher who was going to mentor you backed out of the arrangement. It's not too late to find someone else...and voilà! Here he is!"

"Sil," I say, trying to be patient with my well-meaning friend. "This guy is looking for a woman to race with, not a vet student to mentor."

"So...race with him, and I bet you learn everything you need to know."

"I don't *want* to race with him," I say between clenched teeth. *Take a breath. Be nice.* "I *wanted* to shadow a professional musher for three months and then write a study on the relationship between sled dogs and their owners, and how that relationship informs victory or defeat in competition."

"Right!" says Silvia, banging her desktop with gusto and continuing in a singsong voice. "♫ And if you answer this ad ♫ you can still do that."

I'm done talking about this. It's absurd.

"No."

"Want me to write to him for you?"

I blink at her audacity. "Absolutely not!"

"You're impossible," she says, swiping the magazine off

her desk and jamming it into her backpack.

No. You're *impossible*, I think.

I'm not naïve enough to believe that this conversation is over, but I'm relieved that it's over *for now*. And just in time too.

Professor Steinbuck enters the lecture hall from a side door, placing a folder on the podium centered in the front of the room and opening it to review his notes on today's lesson: The Genetics of Canine Hip Dysplasia.

He's casually hot in jeans and a T-shirt, and I stare at him for an extra second, hoping that his gaze will rise to find mine. Alas, he concentrates solely on the information before him. That's okay. We have a date—er, um, *appointment*—after class, which means I'll have Glenn's full attention later. Yum.

While Silvia chats with the student on her left, I think about my recently dashed hopes for a kickass fellowship, and the fact that I *do* need to formally withdraw from participation by this Friday. It really sucks. Working with sled dogs has been my dream for as long I can remember, and I was thrilled when my proposal won the grant. It hurts to have to turn down the money now.

Growing up as the daughter of a vet in Missoula, Montana, we spent a week up at Seeley Lake every February, volunteering for the Race to the Sky, Montana's biggest sled dog race and an Iditarod qualifier.

My older brother, Braydon, and I would help out the vet crew, mostly, but also assist the mushers in getting their dogs lined up at the starting line and, as we got older, run checkpoint locations along the race and act as vet technicians when needed.

I know a lot about sled dog racing from the veterinary side, actually. The whole point of this fellowship was to learn everything I could about the relationship between dogs and musher, so I could round out my understanding. And the best way to truly comprehend that relationship, I figured, was to live with a musher and his or her dogs for a period of time. To immerse myself in their world.

My father's friend and veteran musher, Steig Nielsen, had agreed to let me spend three months on his ranch, helping at his kennels, and watching him prepare for the 2020 winter racing season. I wrote up my proposal for the Doc Staunton Fellowship in the spring, was notified in August that I'd won the grant, and planned to spend most of this semester in Montana with Steig.

Except...Steig called three days ago to back out of our agreement. A surprise stroke over the summer meant that his health wasn't up to racing this year, and his doctor insisted he take a year off. I quickly reached out to the few other mushers I knew who were located in Montana, but unfortunately, none were comfortable being "under the microscope" from October to January.

So now, even though I have the fellowship grant, and my time away from school's been approved, I no longer have a subject for my project.

It's possible that today's meeting with Glenn might lead to an amended proposal idea, but I don't want to get my hopes up. Besides, with the way my feelings for Glenn have been growing since the semester started three weeks ago, maybe staying in Minnesota this fall wouldn't be so bad.

Just as I think this, Glenn looks up at me, his blue eyes lazy as they slide across my face. I shift in my seat as my body responds to his hot look.

Nope, staying in Minnesota might not be so bad, after all.

***

Knock, knock.

As my knuckles rap on the heavy wooden door, I glance at the brass plaque on the wall: Professor Glenn Steinbuck, DVM, PhD. One day soon my name will have the same letters following it, identifying me as a Doctor of Veterinary Medicine too, and it makes me smile just imagining it: *Dr. Juliet Sanderson, DVM.*

I can hear him inside the office, speaking on the phone, I assume, and knock again.

Knock, knock.

The door opens, but my smile fades instantly as a gorgeous, young female student lingers in the doorway. She leans against the doorframe in her too-tight sweater, her long, dark hair mussed and sexy.

"Thanks, Professor," she says. "For everything."

"You got it, Candace," he says, using the pad of his thumb to swipe at his bottom lip. He clears his throat and grins at her. "I think you'll have a great future in animal husbandry."

"Me too," she hums, her voice low and silky. "Breeding's my favorite."

Glenn chuckles, then notices me standing behind her.

"Juliet! You're here. You're early!"

"Am I? We said three, right?"

Glenn looks at his watch. "And three it is…I guess I sorta lost track of time."

"Bye, Professor," says Candace, smirking at me as she steps out of his office and heads down the hallway.

"B-Bye, Candace," says Glenn, raising his palm in farewell and straining his neck to watch her go.

"Ah-hem."

Glenn's eyes shoot back to me. "Juliet! Yes. Come in. Come in."

I smell it the second I enter the room and pull the door closed behind me: *Sex*. That odd, intense combination of semen, vaginal lubrication, and sweat. Glenn's office windows take full advantage of the late-afternoon sun, so it's hot in here, and every oxygen molecule holds on tightly to the pungent scent.

I'm standing in the middle of a warm, smelly sex cave.

Huh.

It's not that I thought Glenn and I were exclusive, but…

Okay. I guess I thought Glenn and I were exclusive.

Clearly, I am an idiot.

He sits down in the chair behind his desk, and I take a seat in one of the two guest chairs, peeking at it first to see if there are any leftovers from its previous occupant.

"So," I say, letting my backpack hit the floor with a dull thud. "You and Candace."

"Me and Candace…what?"

"You just totally fucked in here."

He grins at me like he's cute. "A gentleman doesn't kiss and tell."

"Is there a gentleman here?"

"That's good." He chuckles. "I like that about you, Juliet."

"My knack for stating the obvious?"

"Your sense of humor. You're sharp. Funny."

"I'm glad I amuse you."

"Come on." He cocks his head to the side. "Don't be mad at me, baby."

"Why would I be mad?" I ask.

"I never said we were getting married," he points out, his eyes lazy under heavy, dark lashes.

"And I never said I wanted to catch an STD," I say, "but I guess I'll get tested after this."

"I use condoms," he tells me, his smile fading a touch.

"Then I guess breeding isn't *your* favorite."

"Okay," he says, leaning forward in his desk chair as he tents his hands on his desk. "You're pissed."

"No," I say, "I'm not pissed." *Yes, I am.* "I'm just surprised."

"Baby," he says, "last I heard, you were leaving town for the next three and a half months. Was I just supposed to wait for you?"

Yes, I want to say. *Yes, you were supposed to wait for me, because we like each other, and I don't just screw anyone. In fact, five minutes ago, before I walked into your office smelling of Eau d'Fuck, I would have called what we were doing over the last few weeks "making love."*

Now the thought of those two words makes me want to heave. We weren't making love. He was fucking me. And I wasn't the only one.

"You're a real class act, Glenn."

He shrugs. Then sighs. Then leans back in his chair, his smile gone, his expression long-suffering. "We weren't in love, Juliet. We just got together a few weeks ago. I thought you knew it was casual."

"I do now," I say, but foolish me, I didn't then. I actually thought that Glenn and I were building something real, something meaningful.

He stares at me for a second, as though waiting for me to say more. When I don't, takes another deep breath, then lets it go. "I guess we should talk about your fellowship."

I want to leave. I really do. I want to walk out of Glenn's office, go back to my apartment, eat a pint of Cherry Garcia and have a quick and dirty pity cry. The *last* thing I want to do is talk about how something else in my life isn't working out the way I wanted it to. I'm embarrassed that I so misread the relationship between us. But Glenn is listed as my official faculty advisor on the grant forms, so he's right; we need to talk.

"I'm sorry your proposed project fell through," he says, picking up small Nerf basketball and bouncing it against the wall of his office.

What a douche.

"Yeah, but technically, I still have the fellowship," I say. "I haven't contacted them yet."

"You need to do that," he says, pausing in his game of catch to look at me. "If you're unable to use the money, they'll need to call their second-choice applicant and let that person know they got the grant."

Not so fast, swift-dick.

Without Glenn's and my romance in play, I find I'm not as eager to stay in Minnesota as I was a couple of hours ago. In fact, I'm downright eager to get the hell out of here. If I never see Professor Stein*fuck*'s cocky face again, it'll be too soon.

"I think there might be another way," I say.

"Your email yesterday said that none of the mushers in Montana would mentor you."

"Yeah," I say. "But I found someone in Alaska that will."

"Alaska."

"Yep. In Nome."

"I didn't realize you knew anyone up there."

I don't, but I'll be damned if I have to show up in Glenn's class twice a week for the rest of the semester. No, thanks.

"I found a guy in Nome willing to work with me."

"A guy? Really?" Glenn leans forward. "You found someone who'll let you live at their place? Be involved with dog care and training? Until January?"

I think about the ad. Nome-o said he was looking for a woman to race with him and that training was available. I assume that he has somewhere for that woman to stay, but if not, I'll use some of my grant stipend to pay for local accommodations.

"Yep."

"What's his name?" asks Glenn, who's been an official Iditarod veterinary volunteer several times, and fancies himself popular among the mushers. Behind his desk, there's a photo of him at the Iditarod starting line in Anchorage. "I probably know him."

"I doubt it," I say. Plus, I have no idea what Nome-o's real name is…yet. "I'll write an amendment to the grant proposal and cc you on the copy when I email it to the board at the Doc Staunton Foundation."

"You don't want to tell me his name, Juliet?"

"Nope. Not really," I say, reaching down for my backpack and slinging it over my shoulder. "And I should probably let you know that I'll be requisitioning a new faculty advisor ASAP."

He tenses. "Are you going to tell them why?"

"Am I going to tell them that you're fucking at least two of your students?" I ask, standing up and pushing the guest chair back under the lip of his desk. "No. I have no interest in being associated with you on *that* level…or on *any* level, frankly."

His shoulders relax. "You know, I'd still love to stay your advisor. This topic is so close to my heart, and as you know, I've volunteered for the—"

"Out of the question."

"Please reconsider."

"Absolutely not."

"Okay. Well…" He leans forward and holds out his

hand. "Part as friends?"

"Fuck you, Glenn," I say, ignoring his hand and heading for his office door. "Fuck you very much."

***

"Oh, my God! Juliet, that's terrible!"

"I know," I tell Silvia.

It's been hours since my final meeting with Glenn, and it still stings that his feelings for me were so…nonexistent. I wasn't in love with him or anything, but he was the first guy in a long time whom I found attractive and exciting. Smart. Knowledgeable. Experienced. Sexy. It turned me on that we both loved animals and wanted to devote our lives to doctoring them. Throw in the fact that he had a soft spot for sled dogs, and I thought we were forever material.

Now I'm embarrassed that I fantasized about us opening a practice together someday or volunteering at the Iditarod together. I feel dirty when I remember the handful of times I slept with him. A twenty-four-year-old student sleeping with her forty-something college professor. What a fucking cliché.

"I'm really sorry, Jules," says Silvia. "I know that girl Candace. She's a total slut."

"Not exactly front-page news, Sil."

"Yeah. Right." Her eyes are sympathetic. "So you told him that you were returning the grant?"

"Nope." I'm sitting at my desk, and Silvia is sitting on my bed with a bag of chips. I turn around to face her, bracing myself for her reaction. "Stay calm, but…I need your magazine. *The Odds Are Good.*"

Chips go everywhere as she throws the bag into the air.

"Oh, my God! Oh, my God! You're going to do it! You're going to write back to Nome-o?"

She runs out of my room, and I hear her racing around our small apartment to find her laptop bag, and there is actually a part of me scared that she'll bang into a wall or pole, like a cartoon character and flatten the entire front side of her body before sliding to the floor. She doesn't. She returns to my room holding the worn magazine like a trophy.

"What are you going to say?" she asks me.

"I don't know," I answer honestly. "But can you vacuum up the chips?"

"Who cares about chips?" she says, opening the magazine to Nome-o's ad and placing it on my desk. She resumes her seat on my bed, her voice going all dreamy as she lies back on my pillow. "Are you going to send a picture? Play up your part as a damsel in distress?"

Um, no.

"I was thinking I'd just be honest," I say with a light shrug. "Tell him I'm a vet student who has a grant and needs a subject. See if he's interested in being that subject."

"Um. No," Silvia says, blinking at me in disapproval. "He's searching for a *partner*, Juliet. He's not asking to be studied."

"Okay. Fine. What's your advice?"

"He's pretty clear about what he wants, Juliet. I think you should say you want to race."

Silvia's cat, Emilio, walks into my bedroom and bunts my legs, marking me with the scent glands in his cheeks.

"Hey, beautiful boy," I say, reaching down to pick him up. His purring intensifies, and he licks the back of my hand with his scratchy tongue.

Cats and dogs are so easy to understand, I think for the millionth time of my life. Bunting, purring, and grooming? A cat showing love. Wagging, whining, and licking? A dog showing love. *How come it's so much harder to read humans?*

"He's going to miss you," says Silvia, reaching for her baby. "Come here, Emilio. Momma's here. Only mean, old Juliet is leaving you."

I transfer the rescue tabby to my bed, and he curls up next to Silvia, still purring, with his eyes at half-mast. She strokes him absently as she purses her lips in thought.

"You can't write that stuff about him being your subject," she says. "If you want him to choose you, you have to be what he wants. You can come clean later...*after* he chooses you."

"That's dishonest."

She sighs, exasperated. "It's a little white lie."

"It's a big, dark-gray lie."

"Not necessarily," she says, her eyes all wide and innocent. "Change your study a little. Learn to race and the study can be about the relationship *you* form with the dogs."

Interesting. It's not a bad angle, actually, but I'd definitely be switching gears.

"I'm not in shape to race," I say, considering it, but unconvinced it's a good idea.

"You swim," says Silvia.

"Only three times a week and mostly for relaxation."

"Will you just trust me? If you want this to work," she says, sitting up, and using a no-nonsense tone, "you need to do it my way."

"Fine," I say, because—*let's face it*—I *do* need this to work. "We'll do it your way."

"Yes!" She jumps off the bed and pushes at my shoulder. "Get up! Let me sit down and work my magic!"

I stand behind her as she cracks her knuckles and gets started.

"Dear Nome-o," she types. "Meet your Juliet…"

CHAPTER TWO

Cody

Dear Nome-o,

Meet your Juliet.

No, really.

My name is actually Juliet.

I'm originally from Montana, where my father is a veterinarian, and for the record, I love dogs.

I'm really intrigued by your ad and would love to know if you're still looking for a woman to race with you. If so, I'm twenty-four years old, in decent shape, and seeking adventure – I think we could be a good team. That said, I don't know very much about sled dog racing, so I'll need to take you up on the training. I can be in Nome by September 30.

Can you also offer a place to stay during training? Or make a recommendation for an inexpensive place nearby?

I'm glad you placed the ad.

Hope to hear from you soon.

Juliet Sanderson

Missoula, Montana

I read the email through, and then start at the top and read it through again.

It's almost too good to be true.

Unlike a few of the other responses I've received, this one includes punctuation, which is a plus. And instead of talking ad nauseam of herself, she speaks specifically to the important points of my ad: She likes dogs. She's young and fit. She's interested in racing and ready to be trained. An additional bonus? She mentions nothing about love or romance. Thank God, because a few responses seemed a little confused—like they didn't notice I'd placed the ad under classifieds and not personals.

I think I've found a winner…and just in the nick of time. The entry form for the Qimmiq Mixed Doubles 200 is due this weekend.

"Wanna 'nother, hon?"

I look up at Rita Beaudoin, the owner and bartender of the Klondike Tap Room. "Yes, please."

She grabs an Alaskan Husky from the fridge under the bar and pops off the cap. "Here ya go."

"Thanks, Rita."

"You're welcome, Cody," she says. It's early at the Klondike, and most of the regulars haven't shown up yet. She flattens her hands on the bar and leans forward a little. "What's gotcha buried on your phone, there?"

"I think I found a partner for the Qimmiq," I say, raising the bottle to my lips and letting the high-octane IPA slide down my throat.

"That right?" she asks. Rita's eyes and hair are dark, like most indigenous folks from Yupik, and if you listen carefully, you can tell from a slight accent that English isn't her first language.

"Maybe."

"Almost missed the deadline." Her eyes slide to the flyer hanging on the bulletin board across from the bar. "Looks like you found her just in time."

"Found who?" Rita's husband, Jonas, sits down on a barstool beside me. "Evening, Cody."

"Hi, Jonas."

"You fixed up that bear cub, Dr. Beaudoin?" asks Rita, opening another bottle of Husky and setting it down in front of her husband.

Jonas, who co-owns the Klondike with Rita, is also the local veterinarian. He shakes his head. "Nope. Both front legs were broken. Had to put her down." He sighs. "Damn these drunk drivers."

"That's a real shame," says Rita, grimacing for a moment before moving down the bar to help another customer.

I don't say anything, but it hurts like hell to hear this exchange. I can't stomach stories about animals suffering or in pain. In fact, I keep my military-issued sidearm in the glove compartment of my truck just for such mercies.

"So, Cody," says Jonas, turning to me, "who'd you find?"

I'm still thinking about that cub. "Sorry?"

"Who'd you find *just in time*?"

"Oh." My cheeks flare with heat, not because I found a racing partner, but because of the way I found her. Lord help me if any of my fellow mushers find out that I placed an ad in *The Odds Are Good*. Classified or not, I'll never live it down. "Um, a girl. For the Qimmiq."

"Ah-ha! Good for you, son!"

The Qimmiq, in its inaugural year, is trying to promote dog sled racing in a new way: as a co-ed team sport. Every team must have two members—one male and one female.

Fun fact: Dog sled racing is already popular with women racers, who often make up 25–30 percent of a race-entry roster, but this race will boast a guaranteed 50 percent female participation rate, the highest on the Iditarod qualifying circuit.

"So," says Jonas, "who'd you get? Brenda Briggs? Jessie Ungalaaq?"

"Juliet Sanderson."

"Never heard of her," he says. "Where's she from?"

"Lower Forty-Eight."

"Wisconsin? Maine?"

"Montana."

"Eh. Race to the Sky country."

"Her father's a vet in Missoula."

"What's his name?"

"Sanderson."

"Sure. Right," says Jonas. "Rings a bell…but I don't think I know him."

I shrug, taking another sip of my beer.

Because I only have five fingers—my thumb and pinkie on my right hand, and my middle, ring, and pinkie fingers on my left—I have to use both palms to lift and hold the bottle, but Jonas doesn't look at me funny. Nor does Rita, for that matter. Neither of them bothers me about my mangled hands and missing fingers. It's part of the reason I like Rita and Jonas so much: because they don't make me feel like a freak.

"So…Juliet, huh? I guess that makes you Romeo?"

Placing that ad was a last resort for me and using a stupid play on words like "Nome-o," to be eye-catching, makes me blush with embarrassment, but finding Juliet—if she's qualified to train with me—will make the whole thing worthwhile.

"I'm no Romeo," I mutter, setting down my beer.

"You're tough on yourself, son," says Jonas.

I rest my hands on the bar, the three fingers of one hand resting on the back of the other. It makes my hands less conspicuous that way.

"I know who I am," I say softly. *And how I look.*

"Someone who got dealt a rough blow."

I was drunk the night I told Jonas my sob story. That was four years ago. I haven't been drunk since.

"I need you to come out and look at Topeka sometime," I say, changing the subject. "I think something's wrong with her right hock."

"Sure thing," says Jonas. "What's your guess?"

"Sprain," I say, "but I'd like to be sure nothing's torn."

"How much is she favoring the left leg?"

"Some."

The door to the Klondike opens, and a group of men step inside the bar. They're unfamiliar to me, and since Nome is such a small town, that means they're probably not from here. It's possible they're gold dredgers or guys from a tanker in port to refuel, but either way, it's my cue to head home. I grab my cap from the bar and mash it onto my head, then slide off the barstool.

"Hey. Stay a bit," says Jonas, glancing at the men. "They won't bother us none."

"Got to get back to my dogs anyway."

I pull my wallet from my coat pocket with my three fingers, steady it between my thumb and pinkie, and pull out a twenty. All of this takes a lot longer than it once did, and I'm trying to move fast, which makes me careless. I drop the wallet on the floor.

"Let me help," says Jonas, hopping off his stool.

"No," I growl, frustrated with myself and maybe even a little bit with him for trying to help when I hate feeling helpless. "I got it."

I reach down and scoop it up with both hands, clumsily shoving it back in my pocket.

"Rita'll get you change."

"I'll get it next time," I say, hiding my hands in my coat pockets. Now that they're out of sight, *my ugly claws*, I feel calmer. I even exhale a breath I didn't realize I was holding.

"Hey," says Jonas, his eyes kind, his voice level. "How about Thursday for me to come out and see Topeka?"

I glance at the group of men, who've taken over two

high top tables at the front of the bar. They're rowdy. Celebratory. I don't begrudge them whatever good thing is going right in their lives. I remember being young.

I also remember being able to make a fist.

"I'd appreciate it, Jonas," I say. "See you Thursday."

"Sure, Cody. See you Thurs…"

I'm out the door and back to the safety of my truck before anyone can touch me.

***

Fun fact: You may start the Iditarod in Wasilla with a maximum of sixteen dogs or a minimum of twelve. No more may be added during the race. And you must cross the finish line in Nome with a minimum of five dogs.

I have nineteen.

Dover, Boston, Juneau, Phoenix, Denver, Augusta, Jackson, Helena, Concord, Bismarck, Salem, Providence, Nashville, Olympia, Cheyenne, Raleigh, Austin, and Topeka are sled dogs.

Viola, a Siberian husky–German shepherd mix, is a retired sled dog and my best friend.

You'd think, with that many dogs, that maybe I wouldn't know each one very well—that the fact that Olympia needs extra behind-the-ear scratches, or Phoenix likes her meat in frozen strips, or Topeka's favoring one leg over another wouldn't catch my attention. But these dogs are my teammates, my friends, and my family.

I love every one of them.

And not one of them gives a shit that I have five fingers on two hands.

That's the thing about animals: they've got their priorities in order. They know what's important—ear scratches, food, doctoring—and what's not. Ten times out of ten I'd choose a dog over most humans I know, and that's the truth.

Except…in this particular instance…I *need* a human.

Of the female variety.

And Lord help me, I don't want to fuck this up. I messed up my dates and missed the entry deadlines on two other races. The female racers I know picked the best male racers in Alaska to be their teammates, and I'm still considered a rookie. I need to make this work with Juliet Sanderson from Missoula, Montana. Why? Because if I don't enter and finish the Qimmiq, I won't qualify for the Iditarod.

And frankly, the most important goal in my life is running the Iditarod in 2020. It's all I've been living for these past five years. I've been training hard with my dogs and gradually upping my races from one-hundred- to three-hundred-mile stretches in preparation for the big one-thousand-mile show.

Poetically speaking, the Iditarod is the sun in my universe, and I'm one small planet circling its glory.

With Viola curled up on the bed beside me, I open up my laptop, click on my mail program and begin the long and painstaking process of typing out a complete message via chicken scratch.

Dear Juliet:

Thank you for your response.

I'm glad you like dogs.

I can teach you how to race.

We need to get started soon.

The race is called the Qimmiq, it takes place in Jan, and it's co-ed.

We race separately; scores are averaged.

I need for us to finish so I can qualify for the Iditarod.

I hope you will take all of this as seriously as I do.

As for a place to stay...

My fingers hover over the keyboard.

A place to stay.

Here's the thing: I could find her a place to stay in town, of course. There are people who'll rent a room. But one, I really don't want anyone in my business, and two, what if she decides she doesn't like staying in town and leaves? If she's staying here, with me, I can do whatever it takes to be sure she's comfortable.

I clear my throat, then reach up and rub the beard on my chin.

Comfortable. Hmm.

Glancing up from my laptop, I slide my eyes around my bedroom, taking it in, trying to look at it, and the rest of my home, from a stranger's po—no, a *strange woman's* point of view. I take a deep breath and let it out slowly.

Houston, we may have a problem...

I bought this land almost ten years ago. A mile north of downtown Nome, I wanted plenty of space to myself where I wouldn't be bothered, where I could live quietly, where I could start over. Once I found the lot I wanted, the rest was easy—the same day I found it, I bought it with cash taken right out of my savings and handed over to the seller.

My house—a modular, two-bedroom, log cabin/chalet-style home—took several months to design, several more months to build in Oregon, another month being shipped to Nome, and another month of actual construction here before I could move in.

But it's lasted me nine winters, and I'm gearing up for a tenth. It keeps the cold wind out and lets the sunshine in. This house may be small, but it's my castle, my sanctuary, and the bones are as solid as they come.

That said…

It looks like a dump, I think, huffing softly.

Viola lifts her head, and I grimace at her. Her ice-blue eyes scan my olive green.

"It's okay, girl," I tell her. "Just sizing things up."

It's been furnished with whatever I could find at church rummage sales, local tag sales, the pawn shop in town, and swap meets. Plus odds and ends purchased at AC's, a local, overpriced, "everything" store, and via Amazon Prime over the years. It's a mishmash of stuff in various styles, most heavily used before it found its way to me.

My queen-sized bed, painted aqua blue? Rummage sale. The scuffed, faux-cherry nightstand missing a brass handle? Tag sale. The bright-green crystal lamp? Local pawn shop. Light-gray area rug with black and red stripes? A Prime Day bargain. The mustard-yellow velvet chair in the corner with a spring just starting to peek through the seat? Traded for lawn furniture I never used. There are no curtains on my windows, and I watch TV on my laptop. A lopsided 8×10 picture of me and my dogs finishing the Copper Basin 300 is the only decoration on one wall, and there's nothing on the other.

Is it cozy? No.

But I don't require cozy. I require a bed to sleep in, a carpet where a recovering dog can rest in front of the stove in my bedroom, and a chair where I can sit down to lace up my boots.

And that's all well and good for me…a single man.

But for a woman in her midtwenties from the Lower Forty-Eight?

It might seem a little rough.

I throw off my covers to inspect the rest of my hovel and hear Viola's paws hit the wooden floor to follow me. To my right is a functional bathroom with a shower, water heater, sink, and john. At the end of the hallway is a great room with an open plan sitting area and kitchen. The sitting area has two mismatched couches covered with blankets and bookshelves so full of books, I've started making piles on the floor. I put my hands on my hips and, best I can, look around through the fresh eyes of a young woman.

It's bleak.

My eyes drift to the far side of the room where a staircase leads upstairs to a loft. Hmm. I probably haven't been up there in a year or more.

Telling Viola to stay downstairs, I climb the steep steps to the loft and stand at the top of the stairs. It's a large room, the length of my kitchen, bedroom and bathroom combined, and has lots of windows, including a huge round one at the apex of the roof. It's about twenty degrees cooler up here, but that could be remedied with a plug-in heater. Over the years, I've used this space for storage, so there's some broken furniture, old dog harnesses, a beat-up Christmas tree and a few boxes, but it wouldn't take more than an afternoon to clear it out. I could order a few things on Amazon Prime to furnish it. A bed, mattress, sheets, and a bureau. Maybe a mirror too. Girls like mirrors.

True, she'd have to go downstairs to use the toilet, but maybe I could figure out how to run a pipe from my bathroom through the floor to the upstairs so she could have a sink. Wouldn't need more than a faucet, basin, and drainpipe to make it happen.

"It could work," I whisper, hustling back downstairs to finish my email and feeling hopeful.

My hand skims along the bannister as I head downstairs, and for a second, for just a few seconds, I can *almost* feel my fingers. All ten of them, like I'm a whole man again.

And then, just as quickly as the sensation came over me, it disappears.

It's like that when you lose a limb—a hand or arm, leg or fingers—you feel them sometimes. On more than one occasion, they've even caused me pain.

I subscribe to the theory that somewhere between my nervous system and brain, there's a sensation misfire. My brain remembers how it felt to be whole and gives my nervous system instructions for all ten fingers. When only five digits receive and answer the call meant for ten, sometimes there's pain, whether psychosomatic or real.

I can tell you this: It feels real. It feels terrible.

When I get to the bottom of the stairs, I hold up my hands and stare at them.

It's been thirteen years, and it still makes me gasp softly. Something inside me wants to believe that it's not true. That it can't possibly be true.

My left hand looks like someone took a knife and cut cleanly from the base of my middle finger to my wrist, hacking off my index finger and thumb. The stump is mostly smooth and even, almost like the fingers never existed at all.

My right hand is much more startling. Grotesquely frozen like a deranged Hawaiian surfer telling everyone to "hang loose," my three middle fingers have ghosted my hand, leaving melted, puckered skin and a flesh-claw in their wake.

How will Juliet Sanderson react to my injuries?

The thought drifts through my head before I can halt it, bringing uncomfortable follow-up questions with it:

Will she look away, disgusted by the sight of my mangled flesh? Or will she feel sorry for me? Will she decide that a man with such a profound physical disability can't be trusted to train her, and inform me that she's heading back to Montana?

Viola, who can sense my changes in mood, whines at me, rubbing her cold, wet nose against my palm.

"It's okay, girl," I tell my dog. "If she takes a look and doesn't want to race with me, I'll drive her to the airport and buy her a ticket home."

I lift my chin with a bravado I don't feel and head back to my room to finish my email.

***

I don't have many friends.

I have even fewer female friends.

I know a few guys on the mushing circuit who I admire and respect, but my only real friends after almost a decade in Nome are Rita and Jonas. They're the only people I really trust, anyway. So the next day, after I feed and exercise my dogs, then move the odds and ends from the loft into the shipping container behind my house, I stop by the Klondike to talk to Rita.

"Cody!" she greets me, her dark eyes twinkling with kindness. "Having lunch here today?"

"Um, sure," I say, though lunch wasn't my main objective in coming into town.

I need to order things for Juliet's room, and I don't know what the hell to get. I need Rita's advice.

She places a menu before me. Without glancing at it, I say, "I'll take a burger with fries and a side of macaroni salad, please."

"You got a summer body, Cody." She tilts her head to the side. "You gotta pack the muscle back on for racing."

Actually, I'm *made* of muscle. Muscle's all I am. If I stood up and lifted my shirt, she'd see the tight cording of a skeleton virtually covered in muscle. I'm sinewy and strong. My dogs and I eat a similar diet of meat, vegetables, and fruit. What I probably need is a little more fat. Muscle alone is not going to keep me warm this winter.

"Okay," I say, "I'll take a slice of pie and ice cream too."

She grins at me, disappears to shout the order at someone in the kitchen, and then returns to set a place for me.

"Uh…Rita," I say, "can I ask you something?"

"You can ask me anything," she says, putting a paper placemat, fork, knife, spoon, and napkin in front of me.

I slide my phone to her, open to my Amazon account. "If you were going to, uh, to decorate a room for a girl…for a woman…what would you buy for her?"

Rita stares at me for a beat. "What woman?"

"The one coming to do the Qimmiq with me."

"Uh-huh. She stayin' with you, Cody?"

"I hope so. I'm waiting for an answer from her, but if she says yes, I want to have everything ready."

"She, uh…she goin' to live with you up there at your place?" Her eyes search my face like she's not sure about this plan.

"Yep." I nod. "She said she needs a place to stay. I can offer her the loft at my house."

"You gotta loft in that house? Ain't never seen it."

"It's nice and big," I tell Rita. I cleaned it out good this morning. It's just clean wood and shiny windows now. "But it's empty. I want to make it nice for her."

Her lips tilt up for a millisecond before she puts on her reading glasses. She picks up my phone. "You want *me* to choose some things?"

"Yeah. If you don't mind. Like, um…she'll need a bed."

"Maybe a good air mattress," says Rita, typing the words into a search bar.

We quickly decide on a queen-sized, comfort-top air mattress with a built-in pump and good reviews.

"You'll need a pillow or two. Sheets…a nice down comforter," says Rita.

"Add it all to my cart."

"What colors you want?" she asks, scrolling through various options.

"I don't care."

"How 'bout sage green? That's nice, right? Neutral?"

"Sure. Green's nice."

Rita clicks on a few items, then looks up at me. "What else?"

I shrug. "I don't…"

"How 'bout an area rug? The floor'll be cold up there, right?"

"Yeah. Good thinking."

Rita's talking more to herself now than me. "…little nightstand. Yep. And a lamp. Uh-huh. Ooo. That's a nice green. Should have a chair for relaxing, probably. Maybe a bean bag sorta thingee…"

"And a plug-in heater," I say.

"Oh, yep. A heater. That's a good idea." She types in something else, nodding at what she finds. "You want her to have a little desk and chair?"

"Probably, yeah," I say. "And a mirror."

"Standing mirror. Check. How 'bout shelves for her clothes?"

"Yeah. Good. How much are we up to?"

Rita swipes the screen and taps twice. "Four hundred and eighty-two dollars and fifty-six cents."

Whew. I can't remember the last time I spent that much money on something that had nothing to do with my dogs…but then I remember: this has *everything* to do with them. Without Juliet, we can't race. Without Juliet and the Qimmiq, no Iditarod.

"Buy it." I blink at her, then clear my throat. "Buy it all."

Rita taps my phone a couple of times, giggles with glee, then places it back down on the bar so I can see the confirmation.

"Free shipping and it'll all be here in seven to nine days. Don'tcha just love Amazon Prime?" She winks at me. "I'll go check on that burger."

As I watch her go, my phone vibrates on the bar to tell me I have an incoming message.

Assuming it's just a confirmation from Amazon, my heart thunders when I see it's from Juliet. This is the moment of truth. Will her answer be yes or no?

I swipe the screen with my thumb and tap on my in-box, holding my breath.

Dear Cody:

Thank you for offering me a place to stay. I accept.

I look forward to learning from you.

You can enter us into the Qimmiq as a team. With

your help, I hope I'll be able to finish.

Please send a packing list ASAP and a street address where I can ship my belongings.

My flight will arrive in Nome at 7:20 p.m. on September 30. I assume you can pick me up at the airport. If not, please advise. If so, see you then.

Juliet

"She said yes," I whisper to myself, a little stunned that my insane plan to find a racing partner in a dating magazine has somehow worked.

It worked! Sweet Jesus, she said yes!

My lips twitch, and I realize that for the first time in a very, very long time, I want to smile. I look around the bar, maybe searching for a friendly face with whom to share my good news, but I'm all alone. That's okay. Maybe it's good that no one witnesses me sitting alone at a bar, grinning like a lunatic on the prowl.

She said yes. Hallelujah.

While I'm sitting there smiling at no one, my eyes slide back to the top of the bar, where my disfigured hands are resting.

I gulp softly, remembering myself.

I didn't tell her about my disability. I didn't want to give her a reason not to come.

Please God, I think, clenching my jaw until it aches, *please give me this one good thing.*

Please don't let the day she arrives also be the day she decides to go.

CHAPTER THREE

Juliet

Ten days.

That's all the time I had to temporarily relocate my life from St. Paul, Minnesota, to Nome, Alaska. Ten whirlwind days that came and went in a rush of shopping, packing, shipping, and good-byes.

Now that I'm sitting on Alaska Airlines flight 153 from Kotzebue, Alaska, to Nome, I can barely remember them.

I look down at the tiny seaside village of Kotzebue as we take off, marveling that an hour ago, I'd never even heard of Kotzebue, let alone considered visiting. I thought this was a direct flight from Anchorage to Nome, so I was surprised when we landed in Kotzebue, deplaned and hung out for about an hour.

During that hour, I learned that Kotzebue calls itself "The Gateway to the Arctic" and is home to roughly three thousand souls, which, incidentally, is the population of Nome too.

Nome…where I'll arrive in about forty minutes. *And* where I'll be spending the next four months living and training with Cody Garrison, my trainer, teammate, and landlord.

Fingers crossed Cody Garrison isn't some psycho ex-con who lures unsuspecting women to his remote cabin outside of Nome with promises of dog sled training, only to murder them in their sleep.

"Anything to drink, miss?" asks the flight attendant.

Just in the nick of time. "Vodka, please. Straight up."

"No mixer?" she asks. "No ice?"

"No cup. Just the bottle. Or two," I say, thanking her when she puts them in my grabby hand.

I unscrew the top of the first bottle and take a big gulp, wrinkling my nose at the burn as the liquor slides down my throat.

To be honest, I don't know why I'm nervous. After I got Cody's full name and street address, I found a reputable detective agency in Minneapolis who ran a background check on him, and they didn't find anything disturbing.

According to the report, Cody Michael Garrison was born in 1985, in Sutter Creek, a suburb outside of Sacramento, California, to a now-deceased father and mother for whom they could not find a current address.

He graduated from high school in 2003, and immediately enlisted in the US Marine Corps. After rising to the rank of Corporal in 2006, he was (*suddenly*) Honorably Discharged from the service.

Of note? He is also listed as "retired," which confuses me a little. Why would he retire at age twenty-one? The only reason I could find, after scouring the internet, is that he was likely placed on the PDRL (Permanent Disability Retired List).

Okay. Fine. But his ad read that he was "fit." So…is the

disability mental? Like, PTSD (Post-Traumatic Stress Disorder) or some other issue that rendered part of him mentally disabled? I thought about asking him over email, but then I reminded myself that for the purposes of the fellowship and my study, it doesn't really matter if Cody Garrison has a mental disability or not. What matters is that he's an active sled dog racer, and he's letting me live at his place during the rigorous three to four months of training prior to racing season.

Anyway, there were no major red flags in his profile. In the thirteen years between leaving the military and now, he has never been arrested, owes nothing on credit cards or in back taxes, has never been married, has no children, claims no dependents, owns his land and home outright, and has placed in the top twenty-five in most of his races.

The next slug of vodka goes down smoother than the first.

The Wi-Fi's free on this flight, so I take out my phone and open an internet browser. I've checked out Cody's musher profile so many times on the Copper Basin 300 website, at this point, when I start typing c…o…p, my browser opens to his musher page, which includes his picture.

Staring at his face, my last gulp of liquor slides down my throat like liquid silk.

Cody Michael Garrison is *hot*.

I mean, I can only see his face, of course, so for all I know, the rest of him is hideous, but his face is *decidedly* handsome.

He's got light eyes—*Green? Blue? I can't wait to find out*—and dirty blond hair with gold highlights. He wears a moustache and beard, the length of which he keeps somewhere between scruffy and bushy. It's thin enough to highlight, not hide, a strong jawline and square chin, which I like in a man.

But it's his lips that make me sigh as I unscrew the top of my second vodka bottle.

I lock on them like a laser on target.

His bottom lip is plush and full, and I know when I meet him in person, my eyes will instantly beeline to it, wondering what it would feel like caught between my teeth.

Cody's lips remind me of Brad Pitt's when he was in *A River Runs through It*, which happens to be my dad's all-time favorite movie. I spent many a night swooning over Brad while my father swooned over fly-fishing.

In fact, it's not just the lips. Cody looks *a lot* like a young Brad Pitt, I think, downing the second bottle of alcohol like momma's milk. He looks like a rugged, angry, messy-haired, unsmiling, bearded, thirtysomething Brad Pitt.

That. Bottom. Lip.

It's so fucking sexy, it makes me want to be inappropriate.

I'm glad I'm staying at his place and he hasn't, as far as I know, murdered anyone in cold blood. Maybe, in addition to being my trainer, teammate, and landlord, Cody Michael Garrison could be—*ah-hem*—something else for me, as well.

(Take that, Professor Steinfuck.)

For the record, I do not think it's a good idea to get

romantically involved—oh, let's just be honest here—*physically* involved with Cody Garrison, but I'm single and he's single, and we're about to spend a few months with each other in a place that's very remote and very, very cold.

I'd be lying if I said that a tryst-on-the-side—*just to keep each other warm, of course*—hadn't crossed my mind.

"Attention, ladies and gentlemen, we have started our descent into Nome. Please stow all carry-on baggage under the seat in front of you and fasten tray tables to their full and upright position. We're landing about ten minutes earlier than expected, despite the soup outside. It's thirty-eight degrees on the ground with light rain. Welcome to Nome, and thank you for flying Alaska Airlines."

I hand my empty bottles to the flight attendant, ignoring her judgey expression, and look out the window as we approach Nome.

It's wet and rainy but still light enough for me to see the landscape.

To my left, the Bering Sea crashes white and angry against the beach as the city of Nome comes into view. The entire town is organized into a grid system, laid out perfectly in about ten north-south streets, and maybe fifteen running east-west. Roofs in red, blue, yellow, and green remind me of aerial pictures of towns in Iceland and Greenland and make me wonder why Arctic towns choose such colorful roofs. Maybe it has something to do with the otherwise drabness of the landscape. From what I can tell, there are no trees and not much natural color aside from the mossy-green of the grass and some brown patches of exposed land.

Gray sky. Gray sea. Gray beach.

Gray roads and gray sidewalks.

Suddenly I wish I'd spent more time sunbathing this summer instead of working inside at my father's veterinary practice.

It's just temporary, I tell myself. *You're only here for a few months.*

We land smoothly, then deplane, and using a rolling staircase, I walk toward the terminal. I drag a hand through my snarly hair, wishing that instead of drinking vodka and mooning over Cody's lips during the flight, I'd brushed my hair or put on some makeup. I woke up at 4:00 a.m. in Minneapolis to catch a 7:00 a.m. flight to Seattle. I've been traveling for eighteen hours. I'm sure it shows.

Fuck it, Juliet. It's too late to primp now.

The terminal is the size of my Minneapolis apartment, so almost as soon as I'm inside, I'm walking through the security turnstile into the main airport terminal. Ahead, there's an Alaska Airlines sign and one check-in desk, and to my right, there's a small conveyor belt where arriving passengers can collect their luggage. Because I shipped all my things directly to Cody, I only have my carry-on backpack to worry about.

I look around the small waiting area for Cody, but he's not here yet.

Hmm. I hope that's not a bad sign.

No, I reassure myself. He's probably just running late. We've corresponded enough that I trust he'll be here to pick me up at some point, and in the meantime, I can catch up on emails and texts from home. I sit down and put my backpack on my lap.

A quick peek at my phone reveals texts from my mom, my brother, Silvia, and Glenn. I'll write back to my family and Sil later. Pursing my lips in annoyance, I swipe open Glenn's message.

GLENN:

I know you probably don't want to hear from me, Juliet, but believe it or not, I never meant to hurt you. I'm sorry. I really would like to stay in touch and hear all about your adventures in Nome. Take care of yourself. Xoxo

The *Xoxo* at the end makes me roll my eyes and sigh loudly. What an asshole. I hate him. Except…I don't. Not totally, I guess, because his words tug at my heartstrings a little too much. I picture the way his eyes crinkled when he smiled at me, the soft touch of his fingers whispering over my skin, the pressure of his hips pressing down on mine, the way it felt when he—

"Juliet?"

My neck snaps up, and my blue eyes slam into Cody Michael Garrison's green.

"Green," I hear myself whisper.

"Excuse me?"

"Your eyes," I say. "They're green."

Because that's the way normal people greet each other: by pointing out the color of one another's eyes. *I'm mad smooth.*

"Yep. Hazel," he says, nodding at me. "You been waiting here long?"

My gaze slides down to his lips.

"Nope," I murmur.

Why, hello, Brad Pitt's doppelgänger. I am happy to report his musher's photo was not air brushed, and he is every bit as hot as I expected him to be.

"Um…are you okay?" he asks.

Shit. I blink at him, standing up from the seat where I've been ogling him. "Yeah. I'm good. I'm—"

I forgot I opened my backpack to take out my phone so when it tumbles from my lap to the floor, everything falls out of it: my iPad, a cherry Chap Stick, spearmint gum, a romance novel I bought in the Anchorage airport, several tampons, a hairbrush, a tangled mess of earbuds and chargers, half a package of dark chocolate almonds, a half-eaten can of Pringles, my passport, my wallet, and a bottle of water.

"Crap!"

I kneel down on the ground, grabbing at my things, trying to keep them from rolling away or getting stepped on.

And what does Cody Garrison do?

Nothing.

Absolutely nothing.

He doesn't squat down to help me, or even pick up something small like my Chap Stick and hand it to me. No. He just stands there, towering over me in jeans, a parka, and ski gloves, staring down at me with this pissed-off expression on his face, like I've thrown the contents of my bag all over the floor for shits and giggles.

Wow, I think, scrambling around on the floor as I shove my belongings back into my bag. *You're an asshole. I don't care how cute you are. Anyone with a little decency would've offered me a hand.*

"Thanks for the help," I say, zipping my bag closed and hauling it up onto my shoulder. My cheeks are red. I can feel the heat in them, a combination of embarrassment and anger.

He stares at me for a second, flexing his jaw once like he's considering offering me an apology. Ultimately, I guess he decides against giving it.

"My truck's out there," he says, gesturing to the parking lot with his gloved hand, then heading toward the exit.

And me? I'm left wondering what the hell I've gotten myself into as I trudge into the parking lot behind him.

***

Cody

When I wear ski gloves, it's almost impossible to tell that my hands are disfigured, which was my big strategy for delaying the inevitable.

I just didn't fucking expect her to drop her bag on the floor and need my help in picking up all her stuff.

So instead of taking off my gloves with my teeth and offering what pathetic help I could, I let her crawl around on the floor by herself.

Fuck. I feel like a giant asshole.

I'm already wondering if this was a mistake, and we haven't even left the airport parking lot yet.

She looks pissed as hell, and you know what? I get it. I asked her up here to be my teammate, and the first time she actually needs my help with something, I stand there like a lump and let her handle it alone.

Great teamwork, Cody.

Shit. Fuck. God damn it.

We are not off to a good start.

She sits down in the passenger seat with a little huff, and I turn over the engine. It's only ten minutes to my house from here, but we'll pass through downtown, so maybe I should order a pizza. We could grab it on the way home. It could be sort of a peace offering.

"You had dinner?" I ask her.

"No," she says, her voice cool. "But I'm not hungry."

"You should eat something."

"No, thanks."

"I can get a pizza," I say.

She doesn't answer, and hell, I can't force feed her. If she doesn't want food, I'm not going out of my way to get something special. I can heat up soup for myself later at home. Whatever.

I take Seppala Drive so she can see a little of the downtown area and try to make a little polite conversation.

"All your boxes came."

"Great."

"I put them in your room. They're, uh, waiting for you."

"Okay," she mutters, crossing her legs away from me and looking out the window.

Her legs are covered with jeans, and she's wearing some cute leather boots with fur sticking out the top. They look warm *and* practical, which is good. But, damn, she's making me nervous. I don't know what I expected—*truth be told, I don't think I ever stopped to wonder what she looked like*—but she's *extremely* attractive.

Almost as tall as me, she's sturdy and athletic, like a strong breeze won't blow her away. I'm guessing she runs or swims regularly because she's obviously fit, though I don't think she's heavily muscled, because her chest is full. It's probably creepy that I checked out her tits, but fuck, I'm a guy, right? And frankly, it's been a long time since I was this close to the pert swell of young, rounded breasts.

Without asking if she minds, I crack my window a touch. It's hot as hell in here.

When I glance over at her, she's still angled toward the window, but now she's got her phone in her hands and she's typing fast. Probably telling one of her friends that her future racing partner is a total jerk and she wants to go home.

Her blonde hair's twisted into a long braid at the nape of her neck, but a few strands have gotten loose around her face. They catch the breeze and curl up next to her cheek, kissing that soft, freckled skin. The light blue fleece she's wearing is the same color as her eyes, and there are tiny diamonds in her ears that sparkle when they catch the dying light.

I'm sure she's regretting her choice to come here.

Fix this, Cody. Fucking fix it or you'll be racing the Qimmiq alone.

"I, uh…" When she doesn't even look up, I feel like an idiot, but I keep going. "I should have helped you out back there…um, at the airport…when you, um, dumped all your stuff out on the floor."

"I didn't *dump* my stuff out. It was an accident."

"I—I know that."

She slips her phone into the backpack at her feet and crosses her arms over her chest, like she's waiting for me to say something else.

"Ummm," I hum, wondering what exactly I'm supposed to say. Maybe I should give her a compliment? "You got it all tidied up real quick."

"Yeah. And you were *such* a big help. Thanks, again."

I grimace, staring out the windshield as I turn left onto Bering Street.

"I'm…I'm sorry," I say softly. "I…It happened so fast…" *Fuck, I'm not good at this.* "I didn't mean to…"

"It's okay," she says, looking over at me, her pinched features finally relaxing.

Wait. What just happened?

"It is?"

"Yeah. Whatever. Forget about it."

The apology, I realize belatedly. *Saying "I'm sorry" made it a little better.*

I've been away from women for so long, I've forgotten how they operate. Hopefully, it'll start coming back to me now.

"Sure you don't want dinner?" I ask her.

"Pretty sure," she says, her voice slightly less chilly.

"They served a snack between Anchorage and Kotzebue."
She pauses for a second, then says, "It's almost eleven
o'clock at home. Honestly, I just want to go to bed, if that's
okay."

"Yeah. Fine."

Thank God for Rita and Jonas, who came over
yesterday. They helped me open all the boxes that arrived
from Amazon, put together the few pieces of furniture that
required a hammer or screwdriver, and Rita set up
everything real nice in the loft. It looks like a bedroom
now—cozy and comfortable—and with the heater running,
it's toasty too. By far, it's the nicest room in my house,
although I did straighten up the rest of the place as best I
could.

I put up some shelves in my living room for the rest of
my books and Rita knew a local gal who made some
matching slipcovers for my two sofas. I bought a cheap,
secondhand TV from the folks at the Seventh Day Adventist
church so Juliet can watch TV in the living room if she
wants. I spruced up the bathroom a little bit too, per Rita's
orders. New towels, and a fully stocked cabinet under the
sink, with tissues and toilet paper and all that nice stuff that
women need.

My room still looks like shit, but she'll never be in there,
so who cares?

I feel good about what I can offer her. I feel like I'm
holding up my end of the bargain.

But when I turn into my driveway and look over at her,
I'm not too sure.

She stares out the window, her face blank, saying nothing, unmoving, and for a second I wonder if she's about to turn to me and shriek, "Take me back to the airport!" but she doesn't.

I follow her gaze and realize she's looking out at the fenced dog yard, where I keep my racing dogs. And, of course, on account of my pulling into the driveway, they're all going completely nuts, howling and barking like it's Christmas morning.

When she turns to look at me, her eyes are sparkling, and I swear to God, I've never seen anything as pretty as Juliet Sanderson in my entire life.

"Those are your dogs," she says.

"Yes, ma'am."

"Can I meet them?" she asks, like she's asking for an audience with the Queen of England.

"Uh…yeah." I nod and gulp. "Of course."

In a flash, she's out of the truck, leaving her backpack behind as she hurries from the driveway over to the dogs.

They're organized in three rows of six, with a separate small area for each dog. There's a stake to which they're chained and a small doghouse with fresh hay where they sleep. They each have a food bowl attached to their house, and their names, lovingly burned into wooden plates, are affixed over the doghouse opening.

Behind their kennels, in the same fenced yard, there is also a grub shack where I store and prepare their food, two snowmobiles, and a golf cart for practicing. In the shipping container where I placed most of the junk from the loft, I keep my practice and racing sleds.

She opens the gate, and I follow her over to the first house, where she stands at a respectful distance from Austin, who stands on top of his house, howling and wagging, hoping for some love from our visitor.

"That's Austin," I say.

"May I pet him?"

"Sure. Yeah. Go for it."

She steps forward in her clean jeans and pretty blue fleece, giggling with glee when he puts his dirty paws on her shoulders to get closer.

"Get down, boy," I tell him, and he minds me, but Juliet is already running her hands through his soft, thick husky fur. I gesture to the dog next to Austin, who's also standing on top of his house. "This is Dover. He's one of my lead dogs."

"Alpha male?" she asks.

I nod. "He is."

"Hi, Dover," she says, letting him sniff her hands before she scratches him under the collar.

"This is Augusta," I say, leading her down the row to the next dog. She shifts her weight back and forth, eyeing Juliet warily. I squat down beside Augusta, hugging her against me as we face Juliet together. "She's a little younger than Austin and Dover. Newer to all of this."

Juliet seems to understand what I'm trying to say: that Augusta may not be as mannerly. She offers her hand to Augusta so that she can smell it but doesn't try to pet her or get in her face.

"I'll win you over, pretty girl," she says gently, and yes, I believe she will.

Cheyenne is standing proudly on top of her house as we approach, but she wags her tail with excitement as Juliet comes closer.

"Miss Cheyenne, meet Juliet. Juliet, this is the pack's de facto momma, Cheyenne." I lean a little closer to Juliet and whisper, "Her vote counts twice."

"Alpha female. Gotcha," whispers Juliet, averting her eyes and bowing her head with respect as she approaches one of my most important dogs.

There is a moment—a very specific moment—when you know that another human is the same kind of devoted dog person that you are. And when Juliet steps forward and offers her hands to Cheyenne before getting a lick on the face, I freeze for a second, waiting to see if Cheyenne's wet greeting will be accepted.

A split second later, with giggles of glee, Juliet's face is buried in Cheyenne's fur and Cheyenne can't lick her new friend fast enough. She's bathing Juliet in kisses, and I'm standing aside, watching these two beings connect on a level that is profound and otherworldly. I'm watching the momma bear of my pack, of my tribe, welcome her newest member.

On down the line we go, dog after dog, with Juliet, who now smells of Cheyenne's approval, being easily accepted by each dog. She asks good questions about a dog's age or personality. She notices things other than pretty markings: if an animal favors one leg over another or seems lethargic. It's dark and frigid by the time we finish our visits with Boston, and by now, most of the dogs are about ready to go into their houses and sleep for the night.

Juliet, in her thin fleece, must be freezing, but she hasn't complained once. I know she's tired too—she said as much in the car, but she's given every dog a few minutes of her time. I'm grateful for the care she's taken in greeting them. More than that, even: I'm impressed.

So it touches my heart almost beyond bearing when she turns to face me and says, "You said you had nineteen dogs. We're missing one."

"Viola," I say, feeling a little choked up by her thoughtfulness. "She's inside."

"Then I haven't met everyone yet," says my new teammate. "Lead the way."

CHAPTER FOUR

Juliet

After a long day of grueling travel and a less-than-perfect first meeting with Cody, the *only* thing that could have brightened my mood is time with his dogs. And meeting those eighteen beauties didn't disappoint. I can't wait to get to know each and every dog better over the next few months, and I thoroughly intend to make Augusta my biggest fan.

I swing back over to the truck to grab my backpack, then follow Cody into his house, which is a cross between a log cabin and a chalet with a covered front porch and warm light beaming from the windows.

As we enter the house, we're greeted by Viola, whom I can see at first glance is an older dog. Her muzzle is gray, and her gait is slow and deliberate. She looks up at Cody with frank adoration and, after sniffing my hand, lets me scratch behind her ears.

"Outside, Vi," he says gently. "Outside, girl. Go ahead."

She lumbers out the door to do her before-bed business as I look around my new home.

I'm standing in a good-sized living room with two sofas covered in some sort of Western zigzag fabric, a coffee table and TV set from the 1990s. A potbelly fireplace in the corner of the room throws off a good amount of heat, and the wall to my left is floor-to-ceiling bookcases, crammed with more books than I could read in a year. Above me is an antler chandelier and exposed log beams. Straight ahead is a small kitchen with a bar area for eating and a staircase along the right-hand wall must lead to a second level.

The windows have no curtains and the floors have no rugs, but the planking beneath my feet is sparkling clean and the curtainless glass is shiny. Cody's no interior designer, that's for sure, but he obviously cares about his home, and I appreciate that.

When he clears his throat from behind me, I look at him over my shoulder.

"You get the upstairs," he says. "Everything up there is, um, new."

"Oh. Thank you."

"My bedroom's back there," he says, gesturing in the general direction of the kitchen with a gloved hand.

I'm relieved to discover that we won't be on top of each other.

Literally…and figuratively.

Whatever silly fantasies I had about us lustily falling into one another's arms for the next three months have disappeared since my arrival.

Cody's good looking, yes, but being late to pick me up and letting me crawl around on the floor at the airport didn't win him any points. He's also a little awkward and very quiet, and while I liked the way he lit up around his dogs, I don't think he's my type. Besides, he's ten years older than I am, and the last time I dated an older man, it didn't go so well.

He does seem to love his dogs, though, and his kennel area was clean, tidy, and comfortable for the animals, which pleased me. I'm sure we'll find our footing with each other, and I hope it includes mutual respect and teamwork. And maybe friendship, if we happen to connect organically on that level too. We'll see.

"Okay. I guess I'll just—Oh! Is there a bathroom upstairs?" I ask.

"N-No. Sorry. Bathroom's over that way too," he says. "By my, um, bedroom."

I nod. *Well, that's cozy.*

Hopefully he's also the sort of housemate who believes in privacy.

Viola scratches at the front door, and he opens it, letting her back inside. She looks up at me with a curious gaze before sitting down beside her master, and the silence between the three of us quickly becomes awkward.

"Well, I guess I'll—"

"You can use the bathroom fir—"

We're talking over each other and both shut up at the same time.

There's awkward, and then there's excruciating. This is becoming the latter.

I take a deep breath. "What were you about to say?"

"You can, um, you know, use the bathroom first…if you want."

"Oh. Sure. Thank you."

Except I'm not unpacked at all. I have no towels, soap,

shampoo, or conditioner. I don't have anything I need to clean up after a long day of travel.

"I'll wait here," he says, crossing his arms over his chest.

"Oh. You mean, you want me to use the bathroom right now?"

He shrugs. "If you want."

"S-Sure." I guess I'll just pee and splash some water on my face for now. I can take a shower tomorrow morning.

My boots scuffle across his clean hardwood floors as I head toward the kitchen. When I get there, I look back at Cody, who points left, so I turn left, down a dimly lit hallway. Pushing open the first door to the right, I find the bathroom.

Like the rest of Cody's home, it's sparsely furnished, but clean, with two snow white hand towels hanging on a rack across from the spotless sink. I sit down and pee quickly, then rinse my hands in the sink. I can't resist the very fresh-looking bar of soap on the side of the sink, though, and use it to wash my face, then dry off with one of the towels that smells brand new.

Did he buy all this new stuff for my arrival? He said as much about my bedroom, so I'm thinking he did, and I'm warmed by his thoughtfulness. I take a moment to look at myself in the mirror—there are dark circles under my eyes, and my hair looks stringy where it's escaped from the braid I plaited early this morning. I look tired. I need sleep.

I turn off the light and make my way back down the short hallway to the kitchen and living room. When I get there, Cody is still standing by the front door, exactly where I left him, with Viola waiting patiently by his side.

"All set?" he asks. "You found the towels?"

I'm too tired to give him a big smile, but my lips tilt up a touch because he's obviously out of his element having me in his house, but he's done his best to make it ready for me.

"Yes. Thanks, Cody."

He nods once. "I also wanted to say...I won't bother you. You don't need to worry about that. For as long as you're here, these are your stairs. No one uses them but you. And up there, that's your space. No one will go up there but you, not even my dogs. I...I just wanted you to know that."

I think it's the most he's said to me in one burst, and for the second time in five minutes, against all odds, he manages to touch me with his thoughtfulness.

"I wasn't worried," I tell him, "but thank you."

He nods again, then drops my eyes. "Well, good night. Come on, girl."

Without another word, he and his dog cross the living room together and disappear down the back hallway.

I blink at their sudden exit, then make my way up the staircase to my right, wondering what awaits me.

As I get closer, I realize that the softest and warmest light in the whole house is coming from "my" space. When I get to the top of the stairs, I halt in surprise and a small gasp passes through my parted lips.

Around the perimeter of the whole room, where the wall meets the ceiling, soft white Christmas tree lights have been loosely braided with sage green tulle ribbon, and pinned to the simple wood molding, giving the entire room a warm, enchanted feeling.

To my right, by the landing, are the four boxes I shipped from Minneapolis to Nome, lined up like soldiers, with a box cutter resting on top for my convenience.

In the middle of the room, under the dramatic slant of the roof, there's a large, comfortable-looking bed made up with light green sheets, two pillows and a thick duvet covered in cream-colored flannel. On the bedside table is a small white lamp with a matching sage green shade, and on the floor is a circular rug so my feet won't hit the cold floor in the morning. Set in front of a large round window, there's a desk and chair, and beside it is a set of shelves for my things.

I drop my backpack on the floor beside the bed and cross over to the desk, looking out the window, and am beyond delighted to realize that my room looks out over the kennel. Only one dog stands atop his house in the moonlight, his breath making puffs of steam each time he exhales. *It's Dover*, I think, the pack alpha, making sure everyone's asleep for the night before allowing himself to finally rest. He is beautiful and proud, and I'm overwhelmed with gratitude for the opportunity I will have to get to know him and his pack-mates over the next few months.

When I turn back around and look at my warm, cozy room, my heart fills with such thanksgiving for this carefully created sanctuary, I feel unfamiliar tears burn the backs of my tired eyes. I don't know why I feel so emotional, and I'm too exhausted to plumb the depths of my scattered feelings, but I do.

In a nook beside my new desk, opposite my bed, there's a sage green and white gingham bean bag with a furry white blanket folded on top.

I fall into it, pulling the blanket around my droopy shoulders and hugging my knees to chest as I cry.

***

Cody

The only thing that separates us is the layer of planking that's her floor and my ceiling.

And there's nothing wrong with my hearing.

It's very quiet, but still audible: she's crying.

Fuck.

She's going to leave tomorrow. I know it.

I sigh with a weariness I barely recognize and sit down on my bed with a heavy heart. Drawing my gloved hands to my mouth, I tug the empty index finger on each, then let them fall from my teeth to the floor. Reaching for my parka zipper with my thumb and pinkie, I pull it down and throw it on my ugly yellow chair.

My hands are sweaty after being trapped in gloves for the last two hours, but I couldn't bear for her to see my claws on the day she arrived. Fuck lot of good it did me. She's up there crying and no doubt planning her escape. I rest my palms on my jeans, letting them dry a little, and wondering where I went so wrong.

Yeah, I was a few minutes late to pick her up because I wanted her room to be perfect and needed to swap out the extension cord for the Christmas lights. And no, I didn't help her pick up her shit because I have *very few fucking fingers*. And she's so young and pretty, which is intimidating for an ugly, maimed guy like me. I know we didn't hit it off, per se, but she seemed to genuinely like my dogs. And I went to such effort to get her room ready and spruce up my house so she'd be comfortable.

I hoped she'd want to stay for a while. I'm crushed that her tears are foreshadowing another possible outcome.

"Fuck," I mutter, leaning down and untie my boots. It's tricky to loosen the laces with the fingers I have, but I eventually manage, taking my time to toe off the thick boots.

Where the hell am I going to find another teammate? I wonder. The answer comes quickly: *You won't. There isn't enough time. If Juliet goes home tomorrow, you can't do the Qimmiq. And if you can't do the Qimmiq, you'll need to wait another year to take a swing at the Iditarod.*

"Fuck," I whisper again, thinking about my plans going to hell.

After five years of learning how to race, nurturing my kennel, getting the right dogs into the right positions and even landing a last-minute teammate for the Qimmiq, 2020 was going to be my year…my first Iditarod.

Except now? It's not looking so good for me.

I reach behind my neck and pull my shirts over my head. It takes time to undo the button on my jeans and pull down the zipper, but I like wearing jeans, so the effort is worthwhile. When I'm standing next to my bed in boxer shorts, I finally hear some movement over my head.

As quickly as I can, I turn off my light and slip under the covers, resting my head on my pillow and staring at the ceiling.

The distinctive sound of packing tape being cut with a knife tells me she's opening her boxes. Then there's the scuffle of her feet back and forth across the floor, from near the stairs to the shelves. Three times. Hmm. Unpacking? I don't want to hope, but I can't help it, I do. I *hope* she unpacks. I *want* her to stay.

After three trips, however, she stops. I don't know what she's doing now, but after about five minutes, the light coming through the floorboards is cut in half, so I think she's turned off her bedside lamp and left the Christmas lights on.

I wait, staring up at the ceiling with breath held, but there's not another peep.

I think she's gone to sleep.

Please don't go, Juliet, I silently pray, staring up at the ceiling. *Please stay.*

I haven't done a lot of praying over the last thirteen years.

Didn't seem like much point. My destiny was decided the day I got my fingers blown off. If God was going to let that happen, He sure as heck wasn't listening to any prayers from me.

And yet, here I am now, praying for something I want. Something that I need.

I can bear the thought of my dreams slipping away when I'm so close to seeing them come true.

When I was honorably discharged from the US Marine Corps in 2006 and placed on permanent disability retirement, I didn't last long back at home in sunny California. With my father passed away, my mother God-only-knows-where, and my much older half-sister settled in the suburbs with a husband and three kids, there wasn't much of anyone to come home to. Most of my high school friends were in college or living their own lives, and the ones who'd stuck around were uncomfortable with how much I'd changed during my three years in the service. I rented a cheap apartment over a friends' garage, watched a lot of Netflix, read the saddest books I could find, and drank my weight in beer.

Three years later, I nearly died. Drunk as a skunk, I almost slept through a fire in the lower garage that should have killed me. It didn't...but only because a stray neighborhood dog stood in the driveway below my apartment, barking her head off until I woke up and saved myself.

I adopted her, named her Viola, temporarily swore off beer, and moved to Alaska.

We ended up in Anchorage for a few years with me occasionally helping out at the VA Medical Center and mostly living off my disability before catching the beginning of the Iditarod race in 2013...and completely falling in love with the sport of sled dog racing. After catching that ceremonial start in downtown Anchorage, all I could dream about was starting a kennel of my own, teaching myself to race, and being one of those Iditarod racers one day.

And now, here I am: one race away from actually qualifying.

My fate lies in the hands of a human being I barely know.

I think about the woman sleeping directly above me and wonder about her a little bit. I don't actually know that much about her. She's from Montana, where her father's a veterinarian, but her boxes were shipped from Minneapolis. Before she dropped all her shit on the ground at the airport, she'd looked up at me with big blue eyes and whispered the color of mine. *Green.*

Huh. I'd forgotten that with all that happened after, be now that I remember, it *almost* makes me smile. It was an odd thing for her to notice, the color of my eyes, but it was almost like she'd been waiting...like she *needed* to know and had finally found out.

Fast forward to arriving back at my place, and it was a pleasure to walk her around the kennel. She was good with my dogs in an organic, effortless way. She took her cues from me with each animal, but I'm guessing her own intuition would've served the same purpose. Some people just have a way with dogs, and Juliet is one of them. She'll be easy to train and a damn fine teammate to me...if only she'll stay.

Please stay.

I sigh softly, picturing her face.

There aren't a ton of single women in Nome, and in my opinion, Juliet is the prettiest woman in town right this minute. She reminds me of the blonde, blue-eyed California girls I went to high school with so long ago. Tan and tall, long-legged and confident. And yes, I know she's a decade my junior, but that doesn't matter. I'm a man. If I was ninety years old, I'd still notice that she's gorgeous. There's no way around it.

That said, I don't have any designs on her, not that it would matter if I did. A long time ago, I gave up on meeting someone, and mostly I've made my peace with it. I have my home and my dogs, a monthly paycheck from Uncle Sam, and an annual oil payment from the great state of Alaska. I have a comfortable life.

I don't need anyone. That's what I tell myself, anyway. That, and: *Some people are better off alone.*

But the reality is a bit bleaker, perhaps: beautiful girls don't want damaged goods. Juliet is fresh and lovely, young and stunning. Any man alive would be lucky to wake up next to a woman like her every morning. *She* has the pick of the whole litter...and *me?* At best, I'm the runt. I'm banged up and bruised, jaded and weary—a virtual hermit, living at the edge of the world, far more comfortable with dogs than people.

I wouldn't dare dream of loving her or being loved by her.

I don't aspire to an impossible destiny.

I'm not a mad man or a fool.

My dreams are much more modest, and hopefully, God willing, still within reach. I want to race in the Iditarod. It's okay if I don't win. I just want the chance to race.

And to do that, I need a partner. I need her.

I pull the comforter up to my chin and close my eyes to sleep.

But before I do, I whisper,

"Please stay, Juliet. Please. Please, stay."

CHAPTER FIVE

Juliet

Stretching my arms over my head, I inhale deeply, taking a deep breath of coffee-scented air.

"Mmmm," I hum, letting my eyes flutter open.

Directly over my head are white twinkle lights, and I blink at them, letting my vision adjust as I remind myself of where I am.

Nome, Alaska. Cody Garrison.

I reach for my phone, charging on the bedside table, and check the time. It's 7:30 in the morning here, but I know my body clock's still on Minnesota time, which means it's really 10:30.

"Wow," I sigh, snuggling under the plush covers. I slept for over ten hours. Impressive. I can't actually remember the last time I slept that soundly.

As I wake up a little more, I realize the sound of excited barking coming from outside is probably Cody feeding his dogs. And shoot, I'm missing it. That said, I've got a lot of early mornings ahead. I'm grateful to be able to sleep in a little bit later this morning.

I never wrote back to my parents or Sil last night, so as long as I have my phone in my hand, I open my texts and send some quick updates.

I tell my parents and brother that I've arrived safely in Nome and that Mr. Garrison has put me up in a comfortable, private room. I promise them I'll send pictures of the dogs later today and stay in touch.

Then I swipe open Silvia's message.

SILVIA:

> **Tell me EVERYTHING. Is he as hot as his picture? Short or tall? In good shape? Did you feel butterflies in your tummy when you met him? How was the condition of his kennel, and do the dogs seem happy? DYING, Jules! Need to know!**

I grin because Sil is so *Sil* about everything, and hit Reply:

JULIET:

> **He is attractive. Tall. In good shape. But there's no spark, Sil. Sorry to disappoint! He seems nice enough, but I don't know yet. Jury's out. His dogs are happy, and the kennel is everything we'd hoped for. He takes good care of them. Anything else?**

I press Send, then click on email.

I have a new message from the University of Minnesota, informing me that my new-advisor requisition has been approved. I will now be working with Sheila Grant, DVM, an associate professor who studied at Colorado State University. I've only had one class with Dr. Grant, but she's not much older than I am, whereas Glenn, for all his shortcomings, was a full, tenured professor with over twenty years of veterinary experience. Oh, well. Beggars can't be choosers, I suppose. I send a quick note to Dr. Grant, asking what she needs from me in terms of project scope and updates, and make a mental note to check for a message from her later.

During my ten days packing and travels yesterday, it weighed on my mind that Cody has no idea that I have ulterior motives for being here. I mean, I'm happy to race in the Qimmiq, if he wants me to, though I don't believe I'll do very well. But my *priority* in being here is to examine his relationship with his dogs and use that data to write a publishable study. Eventually I'll need to come clean and get Cody's permission, but I want to time that conversation carefully. If I mention it too soon, he could refuse to be my test subject, and put me on the next flight out of here. I need to bide my time a little. I need for him to want me to stay just as much as I need to use his life for my case study.

My phone dings in my hand as Silvia writes back to me:

SILVIA:

> **NO SPARK? Come on! He's hot, tall, in good shape, and single! How can there be no spark? I don't believe it.**

My lips twitch as I think about this for a second.

I'm not blind. Cody's not ugly. I might even go so far as to say his face is beautiful, and I'm certain he's covered in muscle. Sled dog racers have to be fit. Biology won't be thwarted, and nature programmed us to have intense attraction sensors and receptors. Is Cody physically attractive? Yes. Empirically.

But that said, he doesn't look me in the eyes when he speaks, and even then, he barely has anything to say. His body language is awkward—head downcast and eyes averted, almost like he's shrinking away from me. For God's sake, he let me crawl around on the floor in a public place and didn't even *attempt* to help me. And yes, his dogs are awesome, and my room is really cozy, which I appreciate, but I guess I just don't feel a connection to him. I don't have a bead on him at all. I don't get him. He's really…uneven.

JULIET:

He's…awkward.

SILVIA:

Like how?

JULIET:

I can't explain it. He's just…not my type. One minute, I think he's an asshole. The next, he seems nice enough…even really nice. I don't know. I just don't think I'm interested.

SILVIA:

You barely know him. Give him a chance.

JULIET:

Nah. Actually, I think it's best if we're just friends. Romance could complicate things.

SILVIA:

You're living in the home of a hot Alaskan

musher. Romance would only make things

more awesome.

JULIET:

Nope. Not happening. Priorities, Sil.

SILVIA:

You are an enigma to me, girl.

JULIET:

I'm okay with that.

I chuckle softly, then put the phone back on the bedside table. When I slide out of bed and my feet hit the floor, I'm grateful for the plush area rug under my feet because I'm sure it's cold as hell outside. The temperatures this time of year in Nome hit an average high of forty degrees and an average low of thirty-four. And it's only going to get colder from here.

Throwing on my terrycloth bathrobe, I gather together some supplies that I shipped here: shampoo, conditioner, body wash, and other toiletries that I'd like to keep in the bathroom, then make my way down the stairs to shower. As I pass by the kitchen, I notice that several large lobster pots are sitting on the now-cooling range, no doubt part of the dogs' morning food preparation. A bright-orange sticky note on the coffeemaker catches my attention. It reads "HELP YOURSELF" in a messy, childlike scrawl.

As I shower, I wonder about Cody.

In my study, I'll need to include a profile on Cody—who he is and how he got that way. So of course I'm interested to figure him out, so to speak. And yet again, I feel some level of guilt that he doesn't know he's my test subject.

"You'll tell him when you're ready," I mutter, stepping out of the shower and toweling off. "You won't *leave* without telling him."

I mean, I wouldn't do that, would I?

I couldn't.

Or…could I?

I use my forearm to unfog the mirror and stare at myself in the glass.

If I used a pseudonym for Cody in my case study, would it be such a big deal if I didn't tell him? I'd be using him for my fellowship, sure, but isn't he using me to qualify for the Iditarod?

Yes, says my conscience, *but he's been upfront with you about that.*

But, really, I counter, *what would it hurt? What harm could it possibly do?*

I mean, if I tell him I'm actually studying him, it could even harm the study; test subjects often change their behavior when they're under the proverbial microscope. He'll be more natural if I don't tell him. And anyway, how would he find out? I highly doubt he reads the sort of veterinary medical journals in which my study would be published.

Shrugging into my bathrobe, I scurry back down the hallway, pouring myself a quick cup of strong black coffee en route to my room.

Usually I would wash and blow-dry my hair at night to get an early start in the morning, so I'm annoyed that it takes a while for me to get my long hair dried and braided. I'm missing out on time with the dogs, when I should be learning their morning routine.

But finally, an hour after I woke up, and bearing in mind it took ten minutes to find my parka and mittens in one of my unpacked boxes, I'm ready to go downstairs and help Cody.

I close the front door behind me, my boots crunching over the gravel driveway as I make my way to the kennel on the northeast side of Cody's property. My stomach gurgles from the acidic coffee sloshing around in my empty stomach, and I briefly consider running back to the house to eat something that'll soak it up but decide to wait. I'd like to see his feeding routine for a couple of dogs, at least. If I don't join him now, I'll miss everything until tomorrow.

He's in the back row of doghouses at this point, already having fed about fifteen dogs. I can smell the dog's breakfast, and from the pungent, gamey smell, I decide it's a mix of defrosted meat, fish parts, kibble, vegetables, and warm water.

I greet the dogs in the first row by name as I pass them, careful not to make eye-contact as I pass by the animals in the second row still eating. They're good dogs, with sweet, social personalities, but food is food, and dogs are protective of what's theirs.

When I get to the last row, I call out Cody's name as I approach him, but he doesn't answer. That's when I realize there are white wires running from his ears. He must be listening to music.

I don't want to frighten him by sneaking up from behind, so I cut through two doghouses, deciding to face him head-on.

He's scooping food into Bismarck's dish when I stop in front of him.

And that's when I see it—*them*—for the first time.

Initially, it just appears that he moves awkwardly, holding the dog bowls against an oil cloth bib over his chest, as he scoops food into the dish. But then I realize:

He's scooping food by fisting a ladle with three fingers.

And he's holding the bowl against his chest with his forearm, which leaves a severely disfigured hand in plain view.

It appears to have—three? No—*two* fingers. A thumb. And a pinky. Nothing else.

My lips part in surprise as I stare at his mutilated hands, and I'm frozen in place as my mind works to add this shocking and vital piece of information into what I already know about Cody Garrison.

He was honorably discharged from the military and placed on a permanent disability list because he's missing half of his fingers, which he likely lost in combat.

He's awkward, most likely, because he not only experienced severe trauma but was left forever damaged, mentally and physically.

And—*fuck me for being a callous fucking bitch*—he didn't help me pick up my stuff in the airport yesterday because he would have had to take off his gloves, which were concealing his mangled hands.

Once-random puzzle pieces snap into place, and I understand more about Cody Garrison now than I've understood in the entire eleven days since we met online, and my heart—my racing heart—swells with sympathy, barely able to comprehend the magnitude of his suffering, of the horror this man has endured.

As I've been gawking at Cody's hands, I haven't noticed the fact that he's stopped what he's doing. Now that I do, I close my mouth, staring at my feet, furiously blinking my eyes to hold back my tears. The ladle slips out of his grasp, and I watch Bismarck's food bowl drop to the ground, empty. The hollow clang of metal on gravel snaps me out of my trance.

Say something, Juliet. You have to say something.

I raise my gaze to Cody's face to find he's staring down at me with a look of such stark dread, such a terrible combination of shame and despair, it makes my stomach flip over.

Combined with the up-close smells of the dogs' morning meal and the way-too-strong coffee that has been assaulting my otherwise empty stomach, I can't prevent what happens next:

Without any warning whatsoever, I throw up the coffee all over Cody's boots.

When I realize what I've done, I gasp in embarrassment, then bolt back to the house like a spooked snow rabbit with a dozen Arctic wolves on its trail.

***

Cody

Stunned is a word.

Another is shocked.

Humiliated.

Dazed.

Put them all together, then multiply them by a thousand, and maybe a new word could be invented to describe the way I feel right this second.

She looked at my hands and—*literally*—got sick.

That's a first, I think, chuckling nervously. But it's a raw, horrible, humorless sound, and Bismarck shifts his weight from side to side and whines.

"N-No," I say softly, leaning down to pick up his bowl. "It's…it's okay, boy. I'm…okay."

That's a lie. *I'm not.*

My hands are shaking, but I somehow manage to pick up the ladle and scoop three cups of stew into Bismarck's bowl before setting it carefully in front of him.

Topeka and Boston are last, and I fill their bowls on autopilot, barely saying a word to them. Then I put the ladle in the stew pot and push the food cart back toward the grub shack. I park the cart in the right-near corner of the shed, then move the massive stew pot to the countertop, covering it for later. I have an electric table saw where I should cut strips of frozen meat for the dogs to snack on during today's workout, but I don't trust myself to use heavy machinery right now.

I pull the feeding smock over my head, hang it on a peg, then lean back against the food preparation counter, trying to take a deep breath though I can't seem to fill my lungs.

She looked at my hands and vomited.

I shove my hands into my parka pockets and clench my jaw, closing my eyes against the burn of unmanly tears. I haven't cried in a long time, but fuck me, I'm *hurting* right now. There's no other word for it.

I hurt.

I bow my head, but images I desperately try to keep at bay come rushing at me. The deafening sound of the explosion. The burned blood that spattered my face, splashing into my eyes and blinding me. The smell of charred flesh. And then—*oh, God, then*—the pain. The *I-want-to-die* levels of pain as I looked down and realized what had happened. The tourniquets wrapped around both of my wrists to staunch the blood, the sirens—

"Cody? Cody, are you out here?"

I open my eyes and reach up with the back of my hand to dry my tears. I'll be damned if I let her see she made me cry.

"Cody? Cody!"

A massive lump sits in the middle of my throat, so I try to clear it, but it won't budge. The sound is enough, however, to lead her to me.

She appears in the doorway of the shed, her body backlit by the bright sun behind her. I can't see her face very well, but that could be because my vision was affected that terrible day, too. I don't see half as well as I once did.

My tattered pride forces me to stand up a little straighter and lift my chin, but I betray myself by shoving my hand, damp with tears, back into my pocket, out of view.

She notices this and winces.

Yes, it's ugly, I think. *Fuck you.*

I'm clamping my jaw together so tightly, it starts to ache, so I loosen it, and I'm finally able to take a deep breath. It's audibly shaky, though. It's ragged and rough. Like the rest of me.

"Cody," she whispers, her voice breaking on my name.

My eyes finally adjust to the dim light, and I stare back at her, saying nothing. There's nothing to say.

She's going to ask me to take her back to the airport, and I will. I won't say a word. I'll sit in my car as she packs, I'll drive her to the airport, and I'll watch her walk inside. Then maybe, for the second time since I moved to Nome, I'll take a seat at the Klondike and I'll order a shot of whiskey. And I'll keep ordering whiskey until I can't smell her puke on my boots, until I can't remember the horror on her face when she saw my hands.

"Cody," she says, "I didn't know."

Maybe I should have told her.

"I didn't think you'd come," I manage to whisper. My voice is raspy and low, and the words I say make my eyes burn with fresh tears because they're so goddamned pathetic. I can't bear for her to see the depths of my sorrow, so I look down at my boots, now stained dark brown from her vomit.

"I would've," she says.

"You would've…what?"

"I would've come," she says. "I still would have come. I just wouldn't have been so surprised the first time I…I…"

Her voice drifts off.

I wish I could feel comforted by her words. Hell, I wish I could *believe* them. But her actions speak louder than her words. She threw up on me when she saw my hands. There's no way we can work together now.

"Yeah," I say, still looking down. "Well, when you're ready, I'll drive you back."

"Back…where?"

To the fucking airport! I want to scream at her. *So you can go home to civilization where people have all their fingers and aren't irreversibly damaged by what they've seen, by the terrible things that have happened to them. You don't belong here with me!*

"Airport," I mutter, stepping forward to push past her and go back to the house where I can bury my face in Viola's soft fur and grieve my broken dreams in the privacy of my bedroom.

I'm surprised when she places a palm flat on my chest, stopping me.

"Look at me," she says softly.

I fucking can't.

"Please, Cody," she says, her voice gentle. "Please look at me."

My jaw is tight, and my lips are pursed in misery when I raise my eyes to hers. But up close like this, so close to her, I can better see the expression on her face. It's not horrified or repulsed. It's sorry. It's kind. It's almost…tender.

Trust is like a vine sometimes, the tendrils reaching out to bridge one living thing to another. I feel a tiny tendril unfurl and bend toward her, reaching for her, wanting so desperately to be anchored to me and attached to her.

"I'm sorry," she says. "I'm so…" She shakes her head back and forth, her lips trembling and eyes full of tears as she speaks. "I'm so sorry."

The lump is back. I try to gulp over it, but I can't.

"I don't know what happened to you, but I'm sorry for it." She clears her throat. Her eyes are so glassy, I don't know how she's keeping her tears from falling. "And I am *so…very…sorry…*for my reaction earlier." She reaches up and swipes at her eyes. "I don't know what happened. The smell of the dogs' food, and the coffee. My stomach was already upset, and I was so surprised—"

"They're like claws," I blurt out. "Unnatural. Repulsive."

Her hand is still flush against my chest, and I don't know if she realizes it—probably not, because I think it's an involuntary, nervous thing—but she's moving her fingers as she speaks. Gently, almost imperceptibly, she's flexing and bending her knuckles, making the pads of her fingers press and flutter against my shirt with each small movement. I can feel the heat of her palm through two layers of cotton, and I imagine my heart straining outward as it beats, hoping she can feel it, hoping she knows that it's there, that ugly people still have feelings.

"No," she whispers, a tear final escaping her eye and sliding forlornly down her cheek. "They're hands. Injured hands. Strange, but not repulsive."

I take a deep breath and give her an "eat-shit" look because I can still smell her vomit.

"Cody. I didn't…*throw up*…because of your hands."

"Sure seemed that way."

She drops her hand from my chest, and fuck me, I instantly miss it.

"No. Not at all. I promise," she says. "I—I've seen more blood and guts in my life than you can imagine. I'm not squeamish."

"How have *you* seen blood and guts?"

"Working with my dad's practice. Plus," she says, "I'm a fourth-year veterinary student. I work at a vet clinic in Minneapolis every weekend."

"What? You're studying to be a *doctor*?"

I can't help the way this comes out, half-disbelieving and half-mocking. But come on. You can't be a vet and throw up every time you see a disfigurement.

"Yes."

"Best get your gag-reflex under control, then."

"I'm telling you…my—" She clears her throat, and two bright spots of hot pink color her cheeks. "—my *reaction* before had nothing to do with your hands. It was the dogs'—"

"—food and coffee on an empty stomach," I finish for her, using her lame excuse.

"I swear," she says, holding up the middle three fingers on her right hand like a girl scout. She glances at her hand and grimaces, like she's embarrassed to have all her fingers because I don't, then she lowers her hand. "Sorry."

"For what? Having fingers?"

"I'm doing this all wrong," she says. "I'm sorry. I'm

just—"

"Can you scoot over? I'd like to leave," I say. "I'll drive you to the airport when you're ready."

But she doesn't budge. She stands there blocking the doorway with her body, holding me captive in the grub shack when I'm getting pretty desperate to leave. My tears are gone now, thank God, but my dogs are expecting a workout and I need to start getting them harnessed. I don't have any more time for this conversation.

"I'm not leaving," she declares, putting her hands on her hips. "I'm staying."

I stare at the challenge on her face for a second, then do something that probably shocks the hell out of both of us: I pull my hands from their hiding place in my pockets, and hold them up in front of her, not three inches from her face.

She sucks in a sharp breath, but I can't see her face because my mangled hands are blocking it.

"It was an IED the size of an ice cube. They told me it was deactivated. They asked me to pack it up for transport. So I did." I pause. "It *wasn't* deactivated."

She gulps softly but doesn't say anything.

"Look at them, Juliet," I tell her firmly, an edge in my voice that surprises me. "Look at them, because if you stay, you're going to see them every day. And you can't throw up on me every time they gross you out."

I lower my hands a little, watching as her eyes stay with my hands, inspecting them. I look for revulsion and horror in her gaze, but this time, I don't see it. I almost *want* to see it—to get this over with and drive her away, out of my life—but it's simply not there.

Her gaze is gentle, almost tender as she caresses my twisted flesh with her eyes. I mark sadness and compassion, curiosity and concern…but I don't see repulsion. Maybe she *wasn't* lying. Maybe her stomach *was* already upset.

After a good sixty seconds, she lifts her eyes to mine, and peripherally, I see her lift her hand to me, holding out her palm between us.

"They don't gross me out, and I still want to be your partner," she says. "Can we shake on it?"

I drop my eyes to her waiting hand, surprised by this gesture. It would be one thing to tell me she's okay with my hands, but she's asking to touch them—to touch the worst of me as a means of cementing our partnership.

I raise my right hand and she takes it, her palm flush to mine, her four perfect fingers clasping the void where three of mine once existed. We hold hands for a while, looking into one another's eyes, and as the moments tick by, I realize she's smiling at me. Her lips tilt up into a small grin, and fuck me if mine don't try to do the same, answering her peace offering with one of my own.

"It's nice to meet you, Cody Garrison," she says, pumping our joined hands gently.

"You too, Juliet Sanderson," I say, realizing, only after she steps aside and finally lets me leave the shed, that she's the first woman who's voluntarily shaken my hand in over a decade.

CHAPTER SIX

Juliet

Three weeks fly by in the blink of an eye when your days consist of a tight, exhausting routine and you were—in no way, shape, or form—physically or mentally ready for it the day you arrived in Nome.

Every day, we wake up at seven o'clock in the morning to start getting breakfast ready for the dogs, though the sun doesn't rise until three hours later and we lose a full six minutes of that precious daylight every day.

We boil two lobster pots of water to help soften the frozen chunks of fish, meat, and fat we feed to the dogs, then mix it with kibble, frozen vegetables, bone marrow, probiotics, and psyllium. Each dog gets three ladles of stew, which means the massive, ten-pound aluminum stew pot gets refilled once, halfway through feeding. The dogs require eight thousand calories a day now, but that'll be increased by two hundred calories a week from now on, until they're eating about ten thousand calories a day in January when racing season starts. That's an insane amount of food, but race dogs easily burn it every day.

After the dogs eat breakfast, Cody cuts about twenty pounds of meat from a frozen block he keeps in the grub shack deep freeze, and lets it thaw all day in water for the dogs' dinner later. Meanwhile, I'm in the house making us breakfast. Most mornings, we have scrambled eggs, bacon, and frozen fruit blended with yogurt into a smoothie. I'm no Gordon Ramsey, but I do my best.

After human breakfast, we harness a team of eight to ten dogs for a day of training. It still takes me about an hour to get them ready, but now that Cody's shown me how, I need to improve my speed for the Qimmiq. My fingers work faster and more nimbly than his, and the extra time gives him a chance to pack dog and human snacks for a day on the trail.

The snow won't start in earnest until early November, and there won't be enough for sledding until after a few major snowfalls, so we still have several weeks before we'll start training with the sleds. For now, we harness the dogs to Cody's golf cart and let them pull us on the seldom-used side roads to the north of Nome. We run them for two or three hours, between twenty and thirty miles, then stop for a snack and a little playtime. After that, we run them back home for another two or three hours. It's not as arduous as the fifty-mile runs we'll do in the snow next month, but it's good exercise for them, and good practice for me.

When we return back to Cody's place in the midafternoon, we take turns mucking out the kennel yard and putting fresh straw in the doghouses, while the other human takes the eight to ten dogs that didn't run to an eight-acre fenced pasture behind Cody's house where they can burn off some energy.

By early evening, we start preparing and ladling out the

dogs' dinner, and by five or six o'clock, Cody's in the kitchen making ours. We sit side by side at the kitchen counter, exhausted from a long, physically draining day, sometimes making small talk about the dogs, and sometimes eating in weary silence.

After dinner, we say goodnight.

I go up to my room to take notes, recording what I've learned that day, and shaping Cody and the dogs into an informative narrative. Most nights I fall into bed by seven, drained to the marrow, and I sleep like the dead until morning.

That's it.

That's my life.

Oh, sometimes I spice it up with an extralong shower in the evening or, when I'm feeling especially ambitious, I'll download a show to my phone or iPad (and invariably fall asleep during the first ten minutes of viewing). But mostly, our routine fills my cup. I don't have energy for anything else. I'm too busy learning everything I can about these dogs before the real training begins…and I love every moment that I spend with them.

Augusta, for instance, finally lets me scratch behind her ears, although she pointedly ignores me while I do.

Topeka, who sprained her hock several weeks ago, is back to full running strength, and she's glorying in her renewed freedom of movement.

Cheyenne treats me like one of her litter, herding me here and there with her nose when we're in the pasture together.

And Juneau, who was initially skittish, rolling onto her back whenever I approached, has learned to trust me and is a cheerful tease.

I'm still getting to know Phoenix, Helena, Salem, and Olympia, but I'm drawn more and more to the female dogs, and I'm wondering how Cody would feel about my having an all-female team at the Qimmiq, with Cheyenne leading the way.

Dover is his alpha male and lead dog, and Cheyenne is generally his swing dog, running right behind Dover and firmly enforcing his rule. I don't know if Cody would be willing to give her up for that race and let her be *my* lead dog. I haven't gotten up the courage to ask him yet.

Since our confrontation in the grub shack three weeks ago after I first saw his hands, we've stayed away from personal conversations, avoiding any intimate conversation, as though by tacit agreement.

We talk about training and racing, and every possible topic related to the dogs, but we don't share our thoughts and feelings about anything else. When we shook hands and became teammates three weeks ago, it's like we reset the clock on our relationship. We're partners and teammates, and as the weeks go by, I find—to my pleasure and surprise—we're damn good at it.

Maybe it's because we're both so intuitive about the dogs, or because we are clear in our roles as mentor and trainee, but we work well together. We put the dogs first, laughing at their antics, celebrating their successes and worrying about them when they seem off. We're coworkers who respect each other, but when the workday is over, so is our relationship. We aren't friends, and so far, I haven't pushed us to become friends.

After dinner, when we retreat to our separate spaces, we leave each other alone. He doesn't come out of his room while I use the bathroom, and I don't ask him if he wants to download a movie and watch it together in the living room. We are separate people living in the same place, working toward the same goals, and mostly, I'm satisfied with it.

No, that's bullshit.

I'm lonely.

And—*shit, I hate to admit this, because I feel like my work here should be enough*—just a little bit bored.

Which is why, as my stamina and strength grow day by day, I start looking beyond the insulated world of my life at Cody's place and start thinking about what there is to do in Nome.

When we drove to Cody's place from the airport, I saw a few bars there and a couple of restaurants. But the question that circles in my mind the most is: if I wanted to go out for a beer, would Cody go with me?

Not that he needs to. I'm perfectly capable of going to a bar on my own. I just…I guess for as much as I haven't *pushed* for a friendship between us, I'd sort of like one. If Cody and I could be friends—could talk about our thoughts and share our feelings, occasionally watch a movie together or go out for a beer—I wouldn't be lonely or bored anymore. I'd have someone. I'd have him.

And Cody seems like a pretty excellent person to have

in your corner. Maybe we haven't talked about personal matters over the past few weeks—and truth told, I think maybe Cody needed a little bit of time to trust me again after what happened the first time I saw his hands—but I have learned a lot about him just by living here with him.

He's gentle, but firm, with his dogs. Patient and encouraging with me. He's focused and ambitious, and good at what he does. Sometimes, when he's in his room, I borrow a book from his massive collection, and I've discovered that his library is spectacularly varied. Yes, there's an emphasis on science fiction and military novels, but he also has classic books, plays, and mainstream fiction. I even found a couple of romance novels in there. There are nonfiction sections of his library on cooking, gardening, and engineering, plus a ginormous area focused on dogs, which even includes some veterinary textbooks.

He doesn't say a whole lot, but I think he's bright. And I like him. As a person. As a partner. In fact, I have grown to like him very much.

Shoot. That's bullshit too.

I think it's possible that I have a little crush on Cody.

Okay, okay. It's *more* than possible.

Christ! Fine.

Here's the truth: as much as I have tried to ignore it, I have definitely developed a crush on him. Why? For every reason I already mentioned, plus the fact that his face is movie-star handsome and his body is so toned, I brace myself when he raises his arms because sometimes, I can see the defined V of muscle that disappears into his jeans. More than once, I've woken up in a sweat, dreaming about that V, dreaming about it pushing against *my* "v" in ways I probably have no business thinking about.

But he's literally given me *zero* encouragement. None. So the leap from my possibly—no, *likely*—one-sided attraction is daunting. I don't want to come off as aggressive by asking him out, but if I never say anything, I'll only have myself to blame if we stay permanently in the friend-zone when there was unspoken potential for something more.

As we sit down at the kitchen counter to eat sandwiches for dinner on a Friday evening, I look askance at Cody, wondering what he'd say if I asked him to go out for a drink tonight and hoping I don't just make a comfortable working relationship awkward by taking the leap.

Hmm. I can be casual, right? Sure I can. Definitely. Casual is in my wheelhouse.

I clear my throat. "So, um… I was just wondering…"

Cody looks up at me, pausing midbite to put his sandwich back down on his plate, then wiping his mouth with a paper napkin as he chews. Something else about the last three weeks: they've allowed me to see how functional Cody is, despite his disability. I'm in awe of how much he can do with half the fingers I have. I'm amazed. I'm consistently impressed.

"Huh?" …but he is not a man of many words.

His green eyes meet my blue, no doubt waiting for me to ask a question about one of the dogs.

"Well, um…I was just…" I clear my throat again.

Casual. We're channeling….casual.

"Yeah…?" He picks up a glass of milk with both hands and takes a long gulp, still looking at me, waiting for me to ask my question.

"Just to be clear," I hear myself say, "we don't need to go out on a date."

He places his glass back down on the table as he blinks at me. "I wasn't aware I'd *asked* you out on a date."

"N-No! You didn't. You never did."

"Did you want me to?"

"Nope! I wanted to ask you."

For fuck's sake, Juliet, this is how you do casual?

"What?" he asks, narrowing his eyes like he's trying to understand. "*You* wanted to ask *me* out on a date?"

"No!" I say firmly, my voice almost defensive. "I wanted to *not* ask you out on a date."

He stares at me for a second, then says, "Mission accomplished."

As he picks up his sandwich to take another bite, I blurt out, "What I'm trying to say…is that I'd like to go out for a drink with you, but it doesn't have to be a date. We can just…drink. An alcoholic beverage. You know, together."

He chews his food slowly, making me wait as long as possible for his reply.

Finally, he says, "Okay."

"What?"

"I will have a non-date drink with you," he says. "In town, I'm assuming?"

"Yeah," I say, surprised that after all my blundering, it was so easy.

"Alright," he says, finishing his first sandwich.

"Really?"

"Sure."

I'm smiling at him. I can feel myself smiling, but I'd know even if I couldn't feel it, because when I smile at Cody, he does this thing where he licks his lips and tugs his bottom lip between his teeth for a split-second, then lets it go. He's such a dead ringer for Brad Pitt when he does it, I've almost said something a hundred times, but held back.

Tonight I don't.

"You look like Brad Pitt when you do that," I say, popping a potato chip into my mouth and feeling excited about my first night out in town with Cody.

He laughs.

It's the first time I've ever made him laugh about something non-dog-related, and when he does, it makes him look about ten years younger. It crinkles his eyes, brightening and softening his whole face, as it sheds a decade of worry. And it sounds like the rumble of deep, beautiful thunder from miles away. Soft and low. It makes me shiver in a good way.

"I mean it," I say, eating another chip as I watch him chuckle.

"You might not believe this, but I used to get that a lot."

"What?" The next chip hovers near my lips. "You did?" He nods. "Yep."

"People told you that you look like Brad Pitt?"

He cocks his head to the side. "*You* just said I did, and

now you're surprised someone else noticed before you?"

"I don't know!" I say, reaching for my water and taking a sip. "Yeah. I guess I thought I was the first person to notice."

"A guy at a mall in Sacramento once asked if I'd be interested in a look-alike job. I guess famous people hire nobodies who look like them to, you know, like, leave from the front door of hotels so they can sneak out the back. Stuff like that."

"You turned it down?"

"I was days away from boot camp." He sighs, his smile completely fading. "I wanted to serve my country. Young and stupid."

"I don't think it was stupid."

"Well…" He pushes his plate away, leaving half of his second sandwich uneaten. "No one would mistake me for Brad Pitt now."

"Nope," I say, wishing his smile would come back, "your hair's still blond and his is gray."

"Yeah. Right," he says, his voice as dry as sand when he plants his elbows on the counter and holds up his hands, palms facing me. "The color of my hair would throw 'em all off."

His hands don't shock me anymore. Not even a little bit. Most of the time I don't notice them, but when I do, I think about his sacrifice: about how a twenty-year-old young man was asked to package up a deactivated IED only to have five of his fingers blown to smithereens.

I rest my elbows across from his and reach up to press

the heels of my palms against the heels of his, slowly closing the distance between our palms until my skin is flush against his. In one pairing, our pinkies and thumbs touch. In the other, our last three fingers.

Part of me is surprised that he allows this intimacy.

And *all* of me is glad that he does.

"I admire you," I whisper, "for so many reasons."

His green eyes, so vibrant and clear, seize mine, holding them, searching them, nearly touching my being through the windows of my soul. Then suddenly, he drops his hands and his gaze, leaving my hands unanchored and alone.

"I'll clear the table," he mutters, standing up and taking our plates to the sink. He deposits them in the basin with a loud clatter. "Dogs are fed. We can go in a little bit."

"Go?" *Go where?* I'm still a little dazed by the intensity of the moment we just shared.

"On our not-a-date to town," he says softly, standing at the sink with his back to me.

I don't know what I did wrong. Or if I did anything wrong at all. But I sense Cody needs a moment to himself, so I leave the kitchen counter and go upstairs to freshen up.

***

Cody

Freud once observed that despite three decades of research into the "woman soul," he still couldn't answer the question: *What do women want?*

Freud, I think, scrubbing our dinner dishes, *I hear you loud and clear, man.*

I can hear Juliet moving around upstairs, and I exhale a long breath. I love having her here, but sometimes I know it's not good for me. And right now is such a moment.

She doesn't want us to go out on a date...but two seconds later, she tells me I look like Brad Pitt.

Three weeks ago, she threw up when she saw my hands...tonight, she voluntarily pressed her palms against mine.

Doesn't she know how dangerous it is for a beautiful woman to be sweet to a guy like me? I could be stupider than stupid and start falling for her, just because it's been so long since a single woman has shown me any kindness.

It doesn't mean anything, Cody, I tell myself. *What looks like mixed signals to you, is just her being herself.*

I mean*, I think.*

No. Fuck that. I know. *I know.* She's not interested in me. She's not. She's just a nice person who gives out nice compliments because it's a nice thing to do. She'd probably be horrified to know that a few kind words could twist around my desperate, pathetic heart and make me wish for things that can never come true.

Once upon a time, when I was a good looking eighteen-year-old kid who'd had his share of sweet, young, high school pussy, I might have had a right to wonder about Juliet's kind words and gentle touches, even with the age difference between us. But that journey ended when I got shipped home. I haven't been laid since, and honestly, I don't really know if I expect to have sex again in this lifetime.

Probably not.

What woman would want to feel my freakish hands on her skin? My burnt, mangled flesh caressing her cheeks or cupping her breasts or stroking the stiff, wet button of her—

"Fuck," I whisper, looking down at my hands, half submerged in dish soap bubbles.

No one. That's who.

And certainly not Juliet Sanderson, who just made it extremely clear that tonight is not a date. It's—*how did she put it?*—two people drinking an alcoholic beverage together. *Oh, the romance.*

I drain the sink, turn on the water, and rinse the dishes before putting them in a drying rack beside the sink. I guess I could change my shirt or jeans, which are both covered in mud, dirt and dog hair, but why should I? I've never changed before when I went to the Klondike for a drink. And Juliet and I aren't on a date, after all.

That said? I have a responsibility to her as my teammate. I wasn't about to let her head into town all alone. Since that fucking show *Bering Sea Gold* started, there are always young guys hanging out in town on Friday and Saturday nights. Thousands of people come to Nome every summer to get rich quick, and when they get drunk together, good manners can sometimes be in short supply. I've shied away from fights because I don't know that I could win anymore, but fuck, I'd figure out how to take a swing at someone if it was Juliet's comfort or honor on the line.

I grab my coat and wallet from my room, then sit down on one of the two couches in my living room to wait for her, trying not to flick my eyes toward the stairs like I'm waiting for a prom date.

But the second I hear her boots on the landing, I'm on my feet, staring up at that staircase like God himself is about to descend from heaven.

And in a way, that's exactly what happens. Except it's not God. It's just His grace in the form of a beautiful girl.

She's changed into clean jeans, a plaid flannel shirt, a bright-maroon fleece jacket and a cream-colored down vest. Her hair, which she always wears in a braid, has been unwoven and falls over her shoulders in long, light-blonde waves. And her face. *Jesus.* I've never seen Juliet wearing makeup before, but her lips are the same color as her fleece, and her eyes are all dark and sexy. She's fucking gorgeous, and she's *here*. In *my* house. With *me*.

For a split-second, I feel like that cocky eighteen-year-old again and remember the long-forgotten pleasure of knowing that a beautiful woman dressed up special just for me.

Halfway down the steps, she grins at me, and asks, "Ready to go?"

Her voice snaps me out of my minitrance.

She's not dressed like this for you, jackass. Get it the fuck together.

"Yeah," I say, shoving my hands in my pockets and looking away from her. "I just need to grab my gloves."

I don't need to grab my gloves. I have no idea why I said that.

I'm nervous, and I have no reason to be.

Non-date, I remind myself.

"I'll wait in the truck," she says, sweeping out the front door and leaving it slightly ajar for me.

After waiting a beat, during which I tell myself that she's my teammate and *nothing more*, I follow her outside, pulling the front door shut behind me.

***

I don't often go to the Klondike after six o'clock, and frankly, I haven't gone to town on a Friday or Saturday night in years, but I still know what to expect. The bar area is full to bursting, and the back room, where there's pool and pinball machines, isn't much better.

On the bright side, however, they'll be gone soon. Aside from needing the snow to do some real training with my dogs, it'll clear out at least half of these guys who aren't interested in being here for a long, cold winter. Fuck, I wish the snow would start now.

Rita sees me walk in from her station behind the bar and gestures to the other side of the room. Assuming there's space to sit down at the end of the bar, I shoulder through the crowd, keeping my head down and only glancing back to be sure that Juliet is following me.

"It's busy here!" she says when we finally get to the two empty seats by Jonas in the corner.

"Yeah. It's popular on the weekends."

"Cody!" says Rita. "Been an age! Wanna Husky?"

I nod, shrugging out of my parka and taking a seat on one of the two empty stools. "Yeah. Two, please, Rita."

"You got it."

Juliet sits down between me and Jonas, grinning at me like she thinks this place is terrific. "What's a Husky?"

"Alaskan beer."

"Oh! Great!"

"How ya been, Cody?" Jonas leans forward, placing an elbow on the bar, so he can see around Juliet. "Doing good out there?"

"Yeah. Good." I flick my chin at the woman between us. "Jonas, this is Juliet. Juliet, this is Jonas. Local vet."

"You're the local vet?" she asks, smiling at him as they shake hands. "I'm a DVM student at the University of Minnesota."

"You don't say!"

She nods. "I'm in my final year."

"Good school, U of M. Went to Colorado myself, though."

"My advisor went to Colorado," she says. "Sheila Grant."

"Can't say as I know her."

Rita returns with the two open bottles and two iced pint glasses. And hand-to-God, before this moment, I didn't even know the Klondike had iced pint glasses. Rita's trying to impress someone.

"Here's your beers," says Rita, holding out her hand to Juliet. "I'm Rita. How'd you like your room?"

"Lovely." Juliet shakes her hand, smiling back. "Did you help Cody with my room?"

"Yep," she says, pouring our beers into the chilled glasses. "I helped him buy all that stuff and get it set up."

"Did you do the white lights?" asks Juliet. "The Christmas lights?"

Rita's brow furrows. "What now?"

"The...lights? And the ribbo—"

I pick up my glass quick and clank it against Juliet's. "Cheers!"

Distracted from her conversation with Rita, Juliet says, "Cheers," before taking a long sip of beer that finishes off the first third of her glass. I can't lie. I'm impressed.

"You *smiling*, Cody? Jesus, I didn't know you had s'many teeth!" cries Rita before whooping with laughter. She grins at Juliet. "Wonders never cease! Ain't seen this one crack a smile in years. You're good for him, *kassaq*."

Rita disappears to help customers, and Juliet turns to me. "What's a guss-ick?"

"A white girl," I tell her. "In Yup-ik."

"Yup-ik?"

"Rita's Yupik," Jonas explains. "Group of Eskimo people that live along the Bering Sea. She's from an island called Nunivak."

"Ah," says Juliet. "Near here?"

"Not so far," says Jonas. "So you're almost a vet, eh?"

She nods. "Yep. I'm doing a fellowship this semester. When I go back, I'll do a thirteen-week rotation at the clinic and then ten weeks at my dad's practice."

"He's a vet too?"

She nods. "In Missoula."

"How you like racing with Cody?"

She turns to me, offering a sweet smile before looking

back at Jonas. "He's very patient. I don't know if I'm a very good student, though."

"You are," I say. "You're doing a great job." I look at Jonas, who's watching us with interest, his eyes flicking back and forth between us like he's figuring out a puzzle. "Dogs love her."

"I bet," says Jonas softly, glancing at Juliet for a longer beat before looking back at me. "Think she'll be ready for the Qimmiq in January?"

"I do," I say, just as Juliet says, "Let's hope so!"

She giggles, clinking her glass with mine, then chugs the rest of her beer. Hot damn, the woman can drink.

"And then back to Minnesota?" asks Jonas, sliding his eyes to my face as she answers.

"Yep," she says. "Spring semester starts on January twenty-first."

I pick up my own beer and finish it off, gesturing to Rita for two more.

January twenty-first. Huh.

The date, which meant nothing special to me before today, sits heavy on my heart now.

I mean, I always knew that she'd leave after the Qimmiq, of course. I guess I just don't like thinking about it. I like her company. I like having her around. I like…her. Aside from the fact that she's nice to look at, I like Juliet Sanderson. She's a good person who loves my dogs, and has tried hard, after an initial fail, to show me that she accepts me exactly for who and what I am. She's probably one in a million, and I only have her near me for three more months.

Still, I tell myself, *that's three more months than I would have had if I'd never found her.*

When Rita brings the beers, I thank her for them, then slide my eyes back to Juliet and Jonas, who are talking about something dog or vet related. My eyes rest on my teammate's shoulder for a second before they skim to Jonas. When they do, I'm surprised to find him looking at me with an expression full of understanding.

He nods his head almost imperceptibly, then refocuses on whatever Juliet is saying.

He knows, I think, breathing deeply as I catch a whiff of her vanilla-scented shampoo, *how much I'm going to miss her when she's gone.*

CHAPTER SEVEN

Juliet

There are levels of drunk.

There's lightly drunk, when you're still pretty much in your right mind, but some of your inhibitions have flown the coop.

There's pretty drunk, when you're starting to get wobbly, but you still remember everything that's happened, you know you need to eat something before bed, and you remind yourself to take two Advil to stave off a hangover.

There's very drunk, when responsibility goes out the window, everything's hilarious, everyone's beautiful, and you can't walk so well but who cares, because it's been the best... night... ever.

And there's so sloppy drunk that you'll barely remember a thing in the morning, the world's about to start spinning, and it would be great if you were near a toilet.

I'm pretty *(very?)* drunk when we get back to Cody's house with a medium pizza to share. I had six beers in two hours, which probably sounds like a lot, but I built up a decent tolerance in undergrad.

Plus, I had the presence of mind to order a pizza from Rita before we left...and I'm sure I have some Advil somewhere.

I plop down on the couch and wrestle my boots off as Cody calls to me from the kitchen.

"What do you want to drink with your pizza?"

"Beer," I say.

"Sure you want another?" he asks. "The dogs will still expect us up by seven, hungover or otherwise."

"Taskmaster," I grumble. Viola jumps up beside me, and I hug her, crooning into her ear. "*You fill up my senses...like a night in the Far East...like a fountain in sunshine...like the talking in Spain.*"

"John Denver's rolling over in his grave," says Cody, putting the pizza box on the coffee table, and placing an open bottle of beer and two glasses of water beside it. After he sits down beside Viola, he picks up a glass of water and takes a sip. "How about some water?"

"No water! I need to sing to Vi," I inform him. "She loves it." I lean back and cup her cheeks, singing earnestly in my very bad voice: "*Like a dorm with a concert...like some Calamine lotion...you fill up my senses...I forget the rest of the words...*"

"The rest?" scoffs Cody, tugging a slice of pizza from the pie. "Try all."

Viola looks at me like I've lost my mind, then jumps down, standing politely in front of Cody and hoping for a handout.

"Why'd you name her Viola?" I ask, picking up the beer and taking a swig.

"Her full name is Viola de Lesseps, the Fire-Frightener."

"Oooo. Fancy." Suddenly, I chortle, thinking of my favorite TV show. "And I am Juliet Montanaborn, the Mother of…" I raise my beer bottle, looking at the canine face on the label. "Huskies."

My hilarious sense of humor is lost on Cody, who clears his throat and says, "Viola de Lesseps was a character from a movie."

"What movie?" I ask, taking a slice of pizza and balancing it on my knee as I take another long sip of beer. Fuck, but I like beer a lot.

Shhh. But I also like Cody a lot.

"*Shakespeare in Love*," he says.

"*Shakespeare in Love*?" I shrug. "I don't know it."

"Gwyneth Paltrow played Viola, and she was…beautiful. Blonde hair like yours. You look a little like her," he says, looking at me thoughtfully before taking a bite of pizza.

"You think I'm beautiful?" I ask him.

"You *know* you're beautiful," he answers, glancing at me with an annoyed expression.

The compliment is grudging, but I'll still take it.

"Hey," I say, nudging his knee. "Did you ever see *A River Runs Through It*?"

He pulls another slice of pizza from the box. "Yes."

"Brad Pitt is in it," I tell him. "I thought you looked like him the second I saw your picture."

There's a short pause, and then he asks, "When did you see my picture?"

"When I was still at home. Your picture is on the

Copper Basin 300 website."

"Is that right?" he asks, turning a little to face me.

"That's right," I tell him, taking another bite of pizza. "Oh, my God! This pizza is *sooo* good."

"You Googled me?" he asks.

"Uh-huh. Of course. I had to see what you looked like…and find out if you ever killed anyone."

His lips twitch. "And what did you find out, Nancy Drew?"

"Murders? Zero. Face? Hot."

"What?"

"You have never been convicted of a murder, and you are extremely hot."

Cody blinks at me in surprise, then sits back on the couch and stares at me. Finally, after a good thirty seconds, he purses his lips and says, "You need to go to bed."

I throw my half-eaten slice of pizza back into the box, grab my beer, and bend my knees so they're under my butt. Then I put my elbow on the back of the couch and stare at Cody just like he was just staring at me.

"You are," I whisper, taking a long gulp of beer, "hot."

He blinks again, his nostrils flaring just a touch, and his pupils dilating. He shifts in his seat, and it makes me want to arch my back and push my tits in his face. Instead, I just grin at him.

"Cut it out," he growls.

"No," I murmur, taking another sip of beer, which cashes the bottle. I lean it against my hip so that my hands are free. "True or false: the Christmas lights around my room were your idea."

He searches my eyes for a second, then nods. "True."

"I love them."

"I'm glad."

"You're hot, Cody."

His cheeks redden. "Stop it, Juliet."

"I'm an adult. I can say what I want."

"You're a *drunk* adult," he points out, "so you should probably shut up."

Here's the weird thing: I know what I'm doing. I know *exactly* what I'm doing.

I'm doing what I've wanted to do for weeks.

I'm making a move on Cody.

"Make me," I tell him, licking my lips as I lean toward him.

With a soft groan, his lips crash into mine, and I fall back onto the couch with him on top of me. My arms wiggle out from between our chests, and I reach up to palm his cheeks as his tongue sweeps into my mouth. He tastes like pizza, which I find delicious, and I suck on his tongue for a second before sliding mine into his mouth too.

He's clumsy, adjusting his body over mine through our layers of clothes, but he's also hungry and intense, and I ride that wave of energy, moaning beneath him as I spread my legs and bend my knees so he can settle between them.

Suddenly, his kiss becomes both gentler and more practiced, like maybe he's remembering how to do this, and out of nowhere, a cache of butterflies releases in my stomach and I feel a surge of wetness between my thighs. Fuck.

Cody's got some moves.

I arch my back, pressing my chest against his, but frustrated by our coats and sweaters and shirts. I want to feel his skin on mine. Right now.

"Your bed," I whisper against his ear as he skims his lips over my jaw and down my throat. "Take me to your bed."

He stops what he's doing but doesn't move.

"Juliet," he says, raising his head so he can look into my eyes. His eyes are so dark, I can barely see the forest in them anymore. They're onyx, like the night sky, fierce and focused. "I don't know if this is a good idea."

"Cody. I want you to fuck me. That doesn't sound *good* to you?"

His breath catches and he flinches. "It sounds amazing."

I push at his shoulders. "Then take me to your room."

"But..." He licks his lips, pulling his bottom lip between his teeth, then letting it go. "We're...partners. Teammates."

"We can be teammates who fuck," I say. "As long as we're adults about it."

"What does that look like?"

"It looks like...having sex," I say. "It looks like...having fun."

"But if it gets all tangled up somehow—"

"You still need me to race the Qimmiq," I say. "Right." I clear my throat, still looking up at him. "Okay. How's this? I promise...no matter what happens between us, I will race the Qimmiq with you."

His tongue peeks out to lick his lips again, and I have a quick flashback to being on the plane, imagining his pillowed bottom lip between my teeth. I pull his face down to mine and bite him lightly.

"Fuck me, Cody," I whisper.

He rolls off me and stands up, offering me his hand…but then, like he realizes he just did something terribly wrong, he yanks it back.

"Fucking give me your hand, Cody," I tell him as I sit up.

We're going to have to overcome this barrier, because it's not going to be much fun if he thinks he needs to hide his hands from me while we're screwing.

He stares at me intently, then offers me a hand, but it's his left this time—the one with three fingers—not the right that he originally offered. Fine. We'll take it step by step.

I take his hand, letting him help me up and lacing my three fingers between his as he leads me back to his bedroom.

When we get there, he lets go of my hand and opens the door, preceding me into the room. It's dark but smells like Cody the same way Stein*fuck*'s office smelled like sex. I close my eyes and breathe deeply: wood fire, dog, the bar of soap from the shower, the spicy deodorant he wears that I've come to love. It all mixes together and smells like…him. It makes me smile.

I hear his coat hit the floor, and I reach for him in the darkness, my hands landing on his shirt. I dispatch the buttons quickly, and he reaches behind his neck to pull off the undershirt beneath.

For weeks, I've wondered about Cody's chest, imagining it tight and hard, with defined muscles built up over seasons of intense racing.

I'm not disappointed.

As I flatten my hands on his chest, over his nipples, I exhale a breath I didn't know I was holding. His skin is warm and smooth as my hands slide down, over the rippled muscle of his chest. I trace the line of his V and sigh. I've been dreaming about what Cody looks like naked, what he'd feel like under my fingers, and I can't lie: he feels amazing.

"All this from training dogs?"

He chuckles softly. I can feel the rumble of it under my fingertips and it makes me wet again.

My fingers stop at the waist of his jeans, and I unsnap the button and pull down the fly, flattening my palm over the bulge behind the V of tiny metal teeth. He's thick and straining under my palm, almost pulsating beneath a thin layer of cotton, and hot against my skin. My heartbeat speeds up. I can hear it in my ears.

He pushes his pants down, and while he does, I throw my fleece and shirt over my head, unhook my bra and unbutton my jeans. Then I stand there in the darkness, waiting for him to touch me.

He doesn't.

Not at first.

"Cody," I say, placing my hands on the warm, smooth skin of his shoulders, "take off my jeans."

I can hear him exhale through his nose as I demand this, but I don't feel his fingers touch down on my waist.

"Cody," I say again, stepping forward and reaching for his arms, "take off my jeans."

I slide my fingers down his arms to his wrists, pausing for a moment before taking his shaking hands in mine. I realize that he's probably frozen at the prospect of touching me, of being intimate with a woman when I suspect it's been a long time for him. But aside from the fact that I'm still a little drunk and horny as hell, I want him to share this with me. I want to be the woman who lets him know that he's beautiful…that *all of him*…is beautiful.

I pull his hands to my waist, skimming them down to my hips. When his hands hit my waistband, I move my hands away, putting them back on his shoulders. My bare nipples brush against his chest and I shiver.

"Cody," I whisper, "take off my jeans. Please."

His trembling fingers dip into the waistband of my underwear, and my breath catches, because there's something intensely erotic about being the first woman he's touched in such a long time. He pauses, as though expecting me to suddenly come to my senses and push him away, so I reach for his face with my hands and pull him down to kiss me. As my tongue slides across the tight seam of his lips, they loosen, opening for me, at the exact same time, he shoves my jeans and panties over my hips.

They pool at my ankles as our kiss deepens, and I step out of them, so that I'm completely naked. Then I wind my arms around his neck, feeling his palms skim over my ass, then up to my waist. He caresses my back, his touches more confident as he wraps his arms around me and pulls me over to the bed. He falls back and I fall on top of him, straddling him, annoyed that he's still wearing boxers, because I want to feel the hot hardness of his cock between my thighs.

Flattening one hand on his chest, I scoot to his side, kneeling beside him. Then I reach for his boxers, pulling them up and over his straining erection. He leans up, so they slip over his ass, then wiggles them down his legs as I straddle him again.

We are naked with each other, skin to skin in each other's arms. His cock slides into the wet folds of my sex, already lubricated by my hunger for what's coming. He is silk pulled tight over muscle and massages the bud of my clit by thrusting gently against it. I moan softly, sitting up, moving my hips in tandem with his.

"God, that feels good." My voice is breathy, and I sigh, leaning forward to kiss him again.

He's strong and quick, though, and flips me onto my back before my lips connect with his, and suddenly I feel the wet heat of his mouth on my nipple, sucking it between his lips and laving it with his tongue, the bristles of his beard a welcome friction against my soft skin. I clench the comforter in my hands as the sensations intensify, letting my head push back into his pillow as he slides his lips to my other breast.

It's been weeks since my body was loved like this, and I arch my back, whimpering softly as he plays with my taut nipples, one covered by his palm, the other by his mouth. His cock slides between my legs, moving slowly over my clit, and my pussy starts clenching because I want him there too.

It's still dark, but my eyes have adjusted enough to see him lean up on his elbows, looking down at me. His eyes are shiny in the moonlight, and they claim mine, holding them for a long moment while his pelvis slides neatly over my slit, his cock rubbing me with smooth, deep strokes.

"I want you," I whisper. "So much."

"I don't have…"

"Condoms?" I pant. "It's okay. I'm on the pill…and recently tested clean."

"Juliet," he says, my name sweet on his lips, "I didn't think…I never thought…"

"You're a good man, Cody." I reach for his face, cupping his cheeks gently. "Don't you know how much I like you?"

He leans down to kiss me, moving his hips so that the tip of his sex is lined up with the entrance of mine. His breathing near my ear is ragged, and his body is trembling, and I wonder if he's waiting for permission from me, or just savoring the moment.

I thread my hands through his thick hair, running my fingers over the muscles in his back, and resting them on his ass. Then grasping at his flesh, I push him forward.

With a deep groan, he slides into my body without stopping, until he is full and pulsating, deep within me, and I cry out at the invasion, welcome though it is. He's big— much longer and thicker than Stein*fuck*—and I have to catch my breath for a second, letting the walls of my pussy relax, then expand as they glove him like a second skin.

"Jesus!" he bellows, his breathing jagged and raw as he pulls out of me, then plunges forward again.

I can feel the strength of his body over mine—the way his arms on either side of my head are planted, not shaking, as he holds his body up, not just resting all of his weight on me. I don't think I've ever been with anyone as physically fit as Cody, and it makes something inside of me surge with primal attraction. My feet slide up the backs of his legs, opening my sex to him completely as he pistons into me.

"Faster," I pant. "More, Cody!"

His hips move faster, his breathing more and more erratic as he rests his sweaty forehead against mine.

"I'm gonna come," he says, his voice breaking over the words as every muscle in a body *made* of muscle tightens so beautifully, I feel like I'm being fucked by a Greek god.

"Come inside of me," I say, tightening my legs around him as that surge within me becomes deafening. My body tenses with his, then shatters, rippling into an orgasm the size and intensity of which I've never experienced. I feel him empty his balls into my pussy in hot, wet streams of cum, and I close my eyes, panting through the extraordinary cocktail of sensations.

I don't know when he rolls us onto our sides, but we're facing each other, still intimately connected, when I open my eyes.

He stares at me, his slick lips tilted up in the most natural smile Cody's ever offered me, and I reach up to trace it with my fingertip.

"Thank you," he says, gently sucking my finger between

his lips before letting it go. "Thank you, Juliet. My God. Thank you."

The evidence of our lovemaking slides in hot streams from my cunt, slippery and wet on my thigh. I don't care. I'll shower when we're done.

And we're not.

Not yet.

Not by a long shot.

After having Cody once, I'm not even close to sated.

I clench my pussy muscles on purpose, as hard as I can, and he gasps.

"More," I whisper, smiling with satisfaction as I feel him start to harden again inside of me.

**

Cody

When I wake up the next morning, Juliet is gone, and if I wasn't still naked, I'd almost wonder if what happened last night was a dream.

But I can still smell the faint scent of vanilla on my pillows, and my body, which hasn't been inside of a woman in fourteen long, lonely years, practically hums with satisfaction. We had sex three times last night: twice in bed and once in the shower, and after that, she snuggled up warm and naked in my arms and fell asleep.

I don't know why she left in the night—maybe she needed more space or maybe it felt too intimate to stay all night. I don't know, but I wish she'd woken up beside me.

I hope she doesn't feel like sleeping with me was a

mistake.

But that thought catches and sticks.

Does she think she made a mistake? Is that why she left? To put some distance between what happened and this morning?

My chest, which was proud and full, deflates like a three-day old balloon.

It's not that I'm in love with Juliet. I'm not.

But I like her.

I like her so much, I feel like if she decides that last night was a mistake, I'll want to die a little. I can't remember the last time anything felt so amazing, so right. But more, I wasn't lonely before Juliet arrived. I had my home and my dogs, an occasional drink with Jonas and Rita. My life may not have been full, but it was good enough for me.

But now? After having her in my arms last night?

How can anything else compare?

How can anything be "good enough" ever again when I've touched and tasted heaven?

I swing my legs over the side of the bed, and stand up, stretching my arms over my head before grabbing some underwear, a pair of jeans, and a flannel shirt. I get dressed quickly, then head into the kitchen where I fill a lobster pot full of water and put it on the stove to boil. I cut the strips of meat from the block last night before we went out, but I have to go out to the grub shack to get them. As I'm pulling on my boots, I hear Juliet's steps on the stairs, and my neck snaps up so fast, it's a wonder I don't get whiplash.

Her hair is braided neatly, and the makeup she wore last

night is gone, but this is the woman that *likes* me, that I fucked three times last night. I'm certain, beyond any measure of doubt, that she's the most beautiful creature on the face of the earth, and I can't help the smile that blooms across my face as I look up at her.

"Morning," she says, her cheeks pinkening as she glances at me.

"Hey," I say.

"Water boiling?" she asks.

I nod. "Yep. Gotta go out to get the pot and strips."

"I already have boots on," she says. "I'll go."

It might be my imagination, but is she acting a little cagey, a little awkward?

I stand up. "About last night…"

"I drank a lot," she says with her back to me. With her hand on the doorknob, she turns to face me. "Sorry I jumped you."

"I wasn't complaining."

"It was fun, but I'm not…" She clears her throat. "I'm not looking for anything serious, Cody. I want to be sure you know that. I don't want to lead you on."

"You're not. You said you were looking for fun." I shrug. "I'm good with that." *Liar.*

"Oh," she says, looking relieved. Her smile seems comfortable, not forced. "Good."

"Good," I murmur, nodding at her as she turns back around and heads out the door.

I'm left alone, wondering what the hell I just agreed to…but the reality is that it doesn't matter. What she gave me last night was so wildly unexpected, so astonishingly generous, my most creative, improbable dreams couldn't have imagined such bounty. If someone had asked me yesterday if I thought I'd ever have sex again with a beautiful woman, I would've given them an unambiguous and categoric no.

And now, here I sit, with brand new memories of her warm skin pressed against mine, her sweet voice whispering in my ear, the small whimpers of pleasure she made when I entered her body, the way it felt when she looked into my eyes and—

"Here we go," she says, stepping back into my house with the ten-gallon stew pot filled with the frozen meat I cut yesterday. She pauses with her back against the door, her eyes meeting mine. "Cody...I'm so full of shit."

"Sorry?"

"All that stuff I just said," she says, gulping softly. "The truth is that last night was a lot more than 'fun,' and I have no idea what I'm looking for, because I can barely get my mind around what we just did."

I can't tell if this is better or worse than her saying she doesn't want anything serious, but I think—*I'm not sure, but I think*—it's better. My heart hardly dares to beat, waiting to see what she says next.

"I have feelings for you," she whispers, her blue eyes wide.

Infinitely better.

"I have feelings for you, too," I answer softly, standing in front the couch, facing her.

"But that's all I know," she says, dropping my eyes.

I cross the room, taking the stew pot from her hands and placing it on a table by the door.

"That's good enough for me," I tell her.

She's only a few inches shorter than I am, but her head is bowed. I lift my left hand, placing my three fingers under her chin and tilting her face up so I can see her eyes.

"I'm all over the place," she says, her eyes glassy and confused.

"I'm not."

I'm right here with you, and it's the only place in the universe I want to be.

Her lips twitch for a second, then tilt up. "Then you anchor us, Cody, okay?"

Us.

It's such a little word. Such a tiny word. Two small letters shouldn't have the ability to make my heart swell with so much tenderness for her, but they do. I haven't been half of an "us" in so long, I'd given up hope of it ever happening again.

And so, for as long as she's here, for as long as she's mine, yes, I'll anchor us. It would be my pleasure. My honor.

"Sure," I say, opening my arms to her.

She steps forward to lay her cheek on my shoulder, and I clasp her tightly against me, closing my eyes in thanks that this woman—despite my injuries and clumsiness—wants to give *us* a chance.

After a minute, she lifts her head and looks up at me with a happy grin on her lovely face. "Hear that?"

I nod at her, unable to keep my smile at bay because wherever we're going, we're going together, and for now, that's good enough for me.

"Dover wants his breakfast," I say, listening to the howls of my alpha and his pack.

She leans up on tiptoes, brushing her lips against mine in a gesture so natural, it stuns me. I'm frozen for a second before my muscles relax and I hold her tighter, kiss her deeper. When she finally draws away, her lips slick from mine, she winks at me.

"Don't keep a hungry man waiting," she says, all sassy-like, heading toward the kitchen, but throwing a teasing grin over her shoulder as she starts preparing their stew.

For a second, I stand still, watching her go, knowing that one day when she walks away, I *won't* be able to follow.

But for now? For today? She's mine.

(I'm our anchor, after all.)

So I do.

CHAPTER EIGHT

Juliet

Here's the thing about having sex for the first time after a night of drinking: you skip a lot of steps. You move too fast, when pacing yourself might've been a better idea.

Cody and I never had a tentative first kiss, or a clumsy first make-out. We jumped from teammates to lovers in the space of an evening, and while the sex was mind-blowing, those skipped steps don't just go away. You still have to figure them out. Because, with every step toward intimacy, new feelings flare up, and each new feeling builds on the last until what you *feel* becomes what you *know*, and that truth exists not on the shaky ground of impulsiveness, but on the rock of deliberate election.

What I'm trying to say is this: having sex too fast can make things awkward.

And this week, I'm experiencing that awkwardness in ways that aren't devastating, but are…a little uncomfortable.

I'm not used to Cody coming up behind me and putting his arms around me.

(Ultimately nice, but potentially hazardous when I jump about a foot into the air.)

He's not used to me leaning up on tiptoes to kiss him out of the blue.

(He freezes in surprise before loosening up, which makes it feel like I'm kissing a marble statue for the first two seconds or so.)

Neither of us quite know what to do after dinner…do we attack each other and fuck? Or do we hug goodnight and go get the sleep we dearly need?

(Tally three nights for amazing fucking and three for excellent sleep.)

And if we *do* sleep, do we sleep together? Does he even want that? Do I? In some ways, sleeping next to someone, all through the night, is almost more intimate than sex.

(Times we've slept together through the night: zero.)

It's been a strange week, I think, leaning over the fenced paddock to watch the dogs play on Friday. Our attraction is a living thing, connecting us through currents of energy that I can almost touch. But we also live together, and work together, and there's a lot we haven't figured out yet.

But I will say this: our conversations, both while working and sharing meals, have become more playful, loaded with innuendo and come-ons. It's the sexy bridge between coming to terms with what we're doing and what we're feeling, and I love it.

"Hey, beautiful," he says, coming up behind me.

I glance at him over my shoulder. "You talking to Cheyenne or me?"

He chuckles. "Cheyenne."

"Dog fucker."

"You kiss your father with that filthy mouth?"

"Yes, I fucking do."

"Got anything leftover for me?"

I jump him. Literally. My arms wrap around his neck as my feet leave the ground, and he catches me, cupping my ass as I lock my ankles behind his back and slam my lips into his. He pivots around, so he's resting his back against the paddock fence, and kisses me back. His tongue is hot and wet, sliding against mine the way his cock slides against the walls of my pussy. Just thinking about it turns me on, and I moan into his mouth, wanting him now, despite the fact that we're outside and fully dressed.

"Can't do it," he says, lifting his mouth from mine, but looking down at me with dark eyes.

"Why not?"

"I have to go somewhere."

Interesting. "Where?"

He loosens his hold on me, and I slide down his body, making note of the bulge in his pants. Wherever he's going must be important, because his cock wants to stay here. I guarantee it's only got one destination in mind.

"Last Friday evening of every month, I take two dogs to the Quyana Care Center over at the hospital."

"Oh! Like, therapy dogs?"

He nods. "Yep. It's good for them to socialize somewhere unusual and be forced to mind their manners even surrounded by a thousand interesting and different smells. And it's good for the patients there."

"Kids?" I ask.

"Nope. Elders. Older folks."

"Wow. That's so nice. I love it."

"It's a win-win for everyone. Dogs look forward to it.

Some of the old guys in there used to race. All of 'em used to have a dog or two."

"Can I come?"

He grins at me. "I was hoping you'd want to."

"You weren't sure?"

He shrugs. "I don't want to make assumptions about you. I just want you to be yourself, so I can get to know the real you. I'd prefer it."

I reach up to cup his face. "The real me would really like to come along."

"You comfortable managing two dogs?" he asks, his eyes twinkling. "If so, we could maybe bring four. You're good with the girls. I mean, you're good with all of them, but you seem to be getting especially close with the girls."

"I am," I say, deciding that this is the right moment to talk to him about something important. "In fact, I wanted to talk to you about racing an all-female team at the Qimmiq."

"You're asking me for Chey?"

"I know she's one of your swings, but I am. She'd be my alpha, my lead dog."

"Okay." Cody nods. "Who would you have beside her?"

I take a deep breath. "Augusta."

"No," he says, shaking his head firmly. "She's not ready."

"I disagree," I tell him. "She's strong, she's young, and she's devoted to Chey."

"Then she should be your swing dog behind Cheyenne."

"She's ready for more, Cody. I know it. I can feel it."

"I believe in following your gut when it comes to dogs." He stares at me hard for a moment. "Okay. Once the snow starts, we'll try it both ways. Gus *behind* Chey, and then *next* to her. If she can handle lead, we'll give it a go."

I start smiling because this means…this means… "I can race the girls?"

He chuckles at me. "You can."

I throw my arms around his neck, hugging him with unrestrained delight. "We're going to kick ass!"

"I pity the other teams," he says, holding me tight.

When I draw back, I capture his eyes with mine. "Kiss me."

His lips touch down on mine, soft and gentle, brushing tenderly. It makes my breath catch, the way this man can be so deliberate, the way he can take his time when he wants to, even after years of deprivation.

He clasps my bottom lip between his, then changes the angle of his head, sealing his lips over mine and seeking my tongue with his. My fingers caress the back of his neck, plunging into his thick hair as he presses me against the fence. The straining bulge of his erection is back now, bigger and harder, pushing intimately against my sex through layers of jeans and underwear.

I want him.

Fuck, I want him now.

"We'll be quick," I promise, taking his hand and leading him to the back of his house.

I open the sliding door to his room and step inside. My

fingers are faster than his, so I unbutton and unzip his pants before mine, but just as my jeans skim over my hips, he lifts me, impaling me on his rock-hard erection without declaration or permission.

"*Fuuuuck*," I moan, licking and biting at his throat as he anchors his hands under my thighs and thrusts into my already pulsing pussy.

He steps to the side and my back hits the bedroom wall, giving him more support as he continues to pump into me. I hold onto him, taking him, letting him thrust as deep and hard as he can while layers of clothing separate every part of our bodies except our faces and where we're intimately joined together.

His fingers dig into the denim covering my legs and I know he's about to come, so I clench his cock as hard as I can, sucking on his neck until I leave a hickey, and crying out with each hard thrust.

He calls out my name, "Juliet! Jul-i-et!"

And then I feel his body shatter all around me, his muscles convulsing as my pussy milks his cock and he drops his forehead on my shoulder, panting against my throat.

"Fuck…" He mumbles through short, ragged breaths. "Fuck, Juliet…Fuck…"

I know he's sated and that makes me so happy I giggle softly.

"Did you…did you come?" he asks, leaning his head up to look at me.

I shake my head with a satisfied grin. "Nah. But it's okay."

"Fuck it is," he says, shuffling awkwardly to the bed, still holding me, the jeans around his ankles making his movements jerky and spare.

His cock slips from my body as he lays me down on my back with my legs hanging over the bed. Then he kneels down on the floor between my thighs, parts the lips of my clit with his fingers, and for the first time ever, he loves me with his mouth.

Stroking me slowly, he keeps his tongue firm, but broad (which I love) and doesn't flick my clit with a fast, pointy tongue (which I hate). He finds my magical bean with ease and puckers his lips around it, then laves it with his tongue. The pressure's good, like he's not scared of the action that area just received, like the tastes and smells of our recent lovemaking are a turn-on, not a turn-off, and soon I stop analyzing the fact that his face is between my legs, closing my eyes and throwing an arm over my head. Because it feels…*good*. No. *N-no*. Oh, my God. It feels…*way better than good*. Cody's got the sort of perfect-porn eating-pussy skills that should make him illegal in several southern states.

Fuck, but this man knows how to love a woman's clit.

I writhe beneath him, my hips bucking up off the bed as I feel my first miniorgasm come and go, leaving tiny tremors in its wake and making me sound off with moans and whimpers.

He chuckles softly—and sweet Jesus, a man has never laughed on my slit while licking and sucking—and I come again.

These are baby Os—lovely but small, like the waves

you consider while surfing, even as you wait for a giant one to sweep you away. My fingers curl into his comforter as he nuzzles my clit with his nose, then kisses it again. His tongue follows in those long, firm, broad strokes, and—fuck me—I can hear my heartbeat start thundering in my ears, or maybe it's my breathing all fast and sharp. I don't know. I don't care. It's so good. *So good.*

In and out…in and out…here we go…fuck…fuck…fuck…

"Codyyyyyyy!" I scream, clenching his head between my thighs as I catch that mega wave and my body explodes into a million pieces, stiff, then writhing, as I ride that beautiful fucking surf, vibrating like a violin string, and cumming like it's the first time.

When it's over, I swear to God, I am a grateful ragdoll—a sated mess of muscleless girl, covered in winter clothes and seeping cum from her slit. I have single-handedly found the golden ring that every woman's reaching for. I just had it in my hand. I can have it again whenever Cody's willing to share it.

I hear him leave the room for a minute, then return, and when he lies down beside me with his legs hanging off the edge of the bed next time mine, his face smells like soap. I roll my head to the side and look at him, smiling like I'm drunk or high or both.

"Where…*the fuck*…did you learn how to do that?"

He grins at me. "I wasn't always like this."

I roll my head back, staring up at the ceiling.

"Were you popular?" I ask. "In high school?"

"Yes," he answers. It's a definitive answer. Absolute.

"Lots of girlfriends?"

"Whoever I wanted," he says, almost dismissively.

"And now?"

"I only want you."

"Was I your first since…"

"I lost my fingers?" he asks. "Yeah."

I roll to my side, leaning up on one elbow, my body still rippling with lovely aftershocks every two or three seconds.

"I'm sorry for what happened to you."

He looks up at me, his green eyes so clear and beautiful, they break my heart a little. "I didn't see it coming. One minute I was whole, the next…I wasn't. The me I knew was…gone."

"Not gone," I whisper. "Just…broken."

"Broken," he murmurs. "Yeah. I was broken. I *am* broken."

I don't say anything. I want him to talk…which means my only job is to listen.

"Did you know Viola saved me from a fire? She saved my life," he says softly, still staring up at the ceiling. "I lived in a loft over my friend's parents' garage, and my friend used to smoke a lot of weed downstairs. One day, he left a joint lit when he left. It started a fire." He clears his throat. "I was drunk upstairs, lying on my shitty couch, and I could smell the smoke, you know? It woke me up, and I had a choice to make." A tear falls from the corner of his eye, sliding into his hair. "I didn't move. I stayed there on the couch. I breathed in the smoke. I…I decided to die."

I am desperate to comfort him, to touch him, to let him

know that I'm a safe place to tell a terrible story, but I don't know what to do. I edge closer, letting the front of my body press gently into the side of his. He doesn't lean toward me, but he doesn't move away either.

"But I could hear barking from down below. Nonstop. Just…loud barking. My landlords had a dog, and suddenly, it occurred to me that he could be trapped inside. You know, downstairs. And I…I couldn't bear the thought of a dog dying too, just because *I* wanted to." He swipes at his eyes with the backs of his hands, then folds them on his chest. "Anyway, I pulled my body off the couch and somehow made my way down the outside stairs. There was smoke everywhere. Thick and acrid. Flames lapping up from below. I could hear sirens but couldn't see the strobe lights yet. Another minute or two, and I would have been trapped. I would've…died." He takes a deep breath and glances at me. "Turns out it wasn't my landlord's dog. It was Vi. She was standing in the middle of the driveway, and when I got down the stairs, she ran over to me, wagging her tail and licking my sooty face. She was a neighborhood stray I'd been feeding now and then. Probably a year old at the time. Maybe younger. She knew I was up there. She saved my life."

I'm so choked up, I can barely speak, but I manage to murmur, "I'm …so g-glad, Cody."

"For a long time, I wasn't." He finally rolls his head to the side to look at me. "I loved Vi for her good intentions, but I wondered if I should have died in Kandahar packing up that IED, or in that garage. I wondered if fire should have gotten me one way or another." He caresses my cheek with the back of his two-fingered hand, staring into my eyes. "A lot of days I woke up and I *wanted* to die." I reach for his hand, turning the palm to my lips, and kiss the scarred skin there. When I open my eyes, he's staring into my soul. "I don't want to die anymore, Juliet."

I freeze, blinking at him.

The implications of this statement—that, perhaps, I am part of the reason he doesn't want to die—are overwhelming to the point of daunting. What if I let him down? What will happen when I return to school? Will he fall apart? Will he want to die again? I can't be responsible for his happiness. Not yet. It's too much too soon.

He must see the play of emotions on my face and continues.

"Oh! No, no. Not because I have forever-plans for us," he says. "But because…after meeting you, I know that being with someone again is…possible. I didn't know that before I met you."

I take a ragged breath, feeling relieved on one hand, but unexpectedly sad on another. Because, honestly, I don't know how I feel about someone else having that sweet forever with Cody. A hot streak of jealousy slides through me like a bolt of white lightning, singeing a path to my heart.

Confusion makes me cloudy, but one thought clarifies quickly through the mist of doubt: a man as good as Cody would have found someone eventually.

I place his hand over my heart. "Forever was *always* possible."

"Maybe," he says. "But I didn't *know* it, until I met

128

you."

And then, because all the words that need to be said for now have been spoken, I draw his body against me, into the comfort of my arms. I cradle him there, anchoring him to me until our barking dogs remind us that there are elders waiting for a visit, and that life, in all its beautiful and terrible forms, must continue.

***

Cody

"Hey, look who's here! *Waqaa*, Cody!"

We walk into the Quyana Care Center, or Quyana House, as it's called by the locals, and some of my favorite folks are hanging out in the small reception area, waiting to greet us.

"*Waqaa*, Ethan," I say, greeting an older gentleman from Gambell. He's wheelchair-bound and frail, but always has a kind word for me and my dogs. "Good to see you. How're you doing?"

"If Travis, here, would stop stealing my dessert at dinner, I'd be golden."

Travis Miklahook, reaching out to offer Dover a scratch behind the ears, gives his cousin, Ethan, a dirty look.

Both Ethan and Travis are Siberian Yupik from St. Lawrence Island, a large island off the coast of Alaska that boasts two towns: Gambell and Savoonga, each home to about seven hundred souls. Closer to Russia (35 miles to the west) than to Alaska (150 miles to the east), both Travis and Ethan are far from home, receiving chemotherapy and radiation treatments at the hospital here in Nome.

The last time I visited, the nurse told me that they likely won't make it back to the St. Lawrence. Each man is in the last stages of terminal cancer.

"You brought four dogs this time, Cody?" asks Travis, his voice raspy and thin.

I've got Dover and Boston on harnesses with one double leash, and Juliet has Cheyenne and Salem on another.

"I've got a helper with me," I tell him.

Ethan looks up at Juliet, then back at me. "No offense, but she's prettier'n you, Cody."

"I couldn't agree more, Ethan."

"How come you got her helping you? Is she your sweetheart?"

Juliet grins at him. "Maybe I should be *your* sweetheart, Ethan."

He chuckles, clapping his frail hands and reaching for Cheyenne, who steps forward to let herself be petted.

A nurse peeks into the room. "Oh, Cody. You're here. Come on back. The residents are waiting for you in the common room."

"You did good with them," I tell Juliet as we head down the hall, forcing the dogs to heel, even though they want to run.

"I love older folks," she tells me. "My grandpa was one of my favorite people in the world."

"You're lucky. I never knew my grandparents."

"What do you mean? They passed away before you were born?"

"Complicated childhood," I say, pushing open a door to our left.

Her eyes linger on my face for a moment before she precedes me into the room where we're greeted by ten of the fourteen Quyana House residents.

Sitting in wheelchairs, in easy chairs or at tables, I know from experience that many of the elders have hidden pieces of sausage or bacon in their pockets, just so they can share a little treat with my dogs. The dogs know it, too: their tails start wagging as they lift their noses in the air and breathe in the smells of breakfast food.

Juliet heads for a group of three ladies, sitting in easy chairs by the fireplace, while I bring Dover and Boston to each wheelchair-bound resident, letting them lavish attention (and treats) on my boys.

Siberian huskies and Alaskan malamutes have a long and treasured relationship with the native people of Alaska, and I am comfortable saying that every elder in this room probably grew up with a dog that looked much like the four visiting today.

Though most Yupik now live in modern homes and drive cars and snowmobiles, it wasn't so long ago that every family needed to have enough sled dogs for transportation. In fact, some of the folks here suffering from Alzheimer's get mixed up and start calling my dogs by old Yupik names from their past…which is actually fine. The dogs couldn't care less, and the elders feel like they've had a visit with an old friend.

While two ladies spend time with Boston, and Dover

gets surreptitious treats from a gentleman in a wheelchair, I look over at Juliet, who's still sitting by the fire. She listens intently to something one of the women is saying—probably *qanruyutet* (wisdom or instruction) in the form of legend or storytelling—while the dogs flank her, their soft fur scratched and petted by Juliet and the other ladies in the circle. After a while, Juliet glances at me thoughtfully, then reengages with the ladies, nodding at them, and finally, letting the lady in the middle kiss the top of her blonde head.

I wonder what they said to her.

Later, when we're driving home in the dark, I ask her.

"They were talking about love," she says, sitting beside me in the front seat of my truck. Dover, Boston, Cheyenne, and Augusta are in the back, happiest with the wind whipping through their thick fur. "She was speaking mostly in Yupik with a little English. She used a phrase that sounded like, um, *ell-u-arr-luc-i pi-ci-qu-ci*. Something like that. It basically means, 'Love well and prosper.' It made me think of the way you care for your dogs." She grins at me. "You're going to win the Iditarod someday, Cody."

My chest swells with pride. "You think?"

"Uh-huh. I know." She pauses. "Something I haven't told you yet about my being here...I have to write a report about my experiences. A paper. It could be published."

"Huh. Wondered what you were doing up in your room at night. I can hear you typing sometimes."

"Does it bother you?" she asks.

"What?"

"To be my subject? You and your dogs?"

I shrug. "Why would it bother me? I'm flattered."

She sighs with relief. "Thanks. I wasn't sure. Not everyone likes being studied."

"Are you *studying* me?"

"To some extent," she says. "You're teaching me about sled dogs: how to care for them, how to race. Yeah. I'm studying you…and them."

"Well, it's fine with me," I say.

Anything would be fine with me, I think, *if it meant you being here beside me.*

"Thank you for taking me with you today," she says. "I really liked it there. Felt good to…I don't know, just to be there, I guess."

"So come back next month," I tell her.

"I'd love t—Hmm. We'll see."

I glance at her. "Why wouldn't you?"

She clears her throat. "My parents asked me about coming home for Thanksgiving."

It's not that I haven't thought about her leaving. I have, of course, but it's always in the context of her leaving in *January*, not before. The realization that I might have less time with her hits me like a ton of bricks, sitting in my stomach heavy and sour.

"Are you going?"

"I haven't decided yet," she tells me. "If I go for Thanksgiving, they'll ask me for Christmas, and that's a lot of time away from, um…here."

I nod once, curtly, because missing her for several days over Thanksgiving and several more over Christmas sounds, well, awful. But it's not my place to tell her where she can and cannot go. And it's not my right to pressure her to spend her holidays with me so early in our relationship.

"What do you usually do?" she asks. "Over the holidays?"

"Um…" I turn into my driveway, rumbling down the dirt and pebble road and stopping in front of my house. "Not much."

"Huh," she says, staring at me for a second like she wants to ask me more questions, but she doesn't. She cocks her head to the side and smiles. "You know what? I bought hot cocoa mix the last time we were in town. How about you put the dogs back in their kennels, and I'll go make us some? It'll be ready by the time you come inside, okay?"

"Okay."

She opens her door and walks into the house, and I get the dogs settled before joining her. When I get inside, she's made a fire in the living room stove, there's country music coming from the phone she's placed on the living room coffee table, and she's in the kitchen stirring two mugs of hot chocolate as she sings along to the music.

My heart.

Oh, my stupid, fucking heart.

It throbs and swells with the warmth of this moment. The fire and the music. The smell of chocolate and her sweet voice in song. But mostly, it yearns for her—for Juliet—to stay and never leave. I don't know what that looks like. I haven't the slightest idea of how to make it happen. And part of me even acknowledges that it never will.

But I want this.

How desperately I want this…forever.

"Hey!" she says, noticing me in the doorway. "Take off your coat. It's almost ready."

I unzip my parka, then bend down to unlace my boots. I toe them off, leaving them on a mat beside the front door, and hang up my coat on the rack beside the mat, next to hers.

She comes out of the kitchen, blonde braid sitting pretty over one shoulder, and warm smile making me want things I shouldn't even wish for.

She's going back to college after the Qimmiq, I tell myself. *You always knew that.*

After placing the mugs on the coffee table, she pats the cushion next to her. "Come sit with me."

Because her wish is, and likely will always be, my command, I cross over to the sofa and sit down. She puts her feet up on the coffee table and her head on my shoulder. I lean forward to take my mug carefully, then think twice and decide to leave it until it cools. Unlike people with all their fingers, it's hard for me to hold a mug. It's best if I can hold mugs and glasses firmly between both palms, but the ceramic is too hot to hold flush against my skin right now.

"Don't want it?" she asks.

"I'll drink it in a bit."

She's quiet for a second, then says, "Tell me about Thanksgiving and Christmas, Cody."

"There isn't much to tell," I say, pulling a blanket of the back of the couch and covering our laps with it. "Sometimes

Jonas and Rita invite me to spend Thanksgiving with them. But sometimes they spend it with their son, Mitchell, down in Juneau. One year I took a couple of the dogs over to the Quyana House. They invited me to stay for supper."

"How about Christmas?" she asks.

"Last year we took a long ride," I say. "Maybe six hours. We were tired out by the time we got back."

Her breath releases in a small "ahh" sound, and I don't know what that means, but I suspect my holidays sound pretty awful. Not much to entice her to stay.

"Remember earlier today?" she says. "When I asked about your grandparents? What did you mean when you said you never knew them?"

I really don't like talking about this stuff. "What are you trying to get at here?"

"I want to know you," she says. "I want to know…why you don't know your grandparents…why you live all alone here in Nome…why you don't celebrate major holidays."

I sigh audibly, but she doesn't retract her questions. And frankly, I guess it's my fault for mentioning the fact that I have no grandparents in the first place. I inadvertently piqued her curiosity. So I guess I should take responsibility for that and just tell my whole sad story in one fell swoop.

"Fine. You want my story? Here it is. My parents weren't married. My mother was an exotic dancer in Rancho Cordova, outside of Sacramento. My father was a salesman with a wife and daughter in Fresno. I only saw my father once or twice a year, and never met my half-sister until his funeral, when I was fifteen."

"Whew," she says softly, sipping her chocolate, but keeping her head on my shoulder. "Are you still in touch with her?"

"Sort of," I say. "She's on Facebook. We exchange messages every so often."

"What about your mom?"

"She was originally from Florida and always said she was an orphan, which may have been true. When I was in middle school, I remember a guy coming around now and then who she said was her 'foster brother,' so maybe she *was* an orphan. I don't know. We never heard from anyone. Never visited anyone. Nothing. Anyway...from the time I was sixteen, she was at home less and less often. A night here. Two days there. Then one day, she never came home at all."

Juliet gasps softly. "What? What do you mean? She *abandoned* you?"

"No, it wasn't really like that."

"If she left when you were sixteen and never came back, that's *exactly* what it was like."

"It was better after she left," I tell her. "She called from a pay phone to say she'd relocated to Vegas and I was old enough to fend for myself. She'd paid up the rent for six months, so I got a job after school and on weekends, banked every dime and was able to make ends meet until I entered the service."

"Cody," she says softly, burrowing closer to me. "That's *terrible*."

Honestly? It really *wasn't* that terrible. I was young to be on my own, but it was a relief not to worry about her anymore. I could imagine her having the time of her life in Vegas, while I finished up the last two years of high school with lots of freedom. It could have been worse.

"Do you ever hear from her?"

"Not much." I shrug. "She's on Facebook, too. Pops up every so often and sends me a message. Mostly on my birthday."

"When's your birthday?"

"June."

We sit there in the dim light of the fire, with Vi at our feet and Juliet's head on my shoulder. My chocolate's probably cool by now, but I don't want to move. The blanket's warm, and the woman's soft, and telling her my hard-luck story didn't make me feel as pathetic as I expected it to. She's a good listener. Just another thing to love about her.

I don't know how long we sit together, but when I hear her softly snoring, I nudge her.

"Hey, beautiful," I whisper. "It's time for bed."

"Mmm," she hums, breathing deeply and nestling closer.

"Hey…Juliet…" I say, but she doesn't move. She's sleeping soundly, and I don't have the heart to wake her up. I stand up without waking her, then scoop her into my arms, blanket and all.

I walk to the back hallway with Vi at my heels, push open the door to my bedroom with a socked foot, and deposit Juliet gently onto my bed.

Still dressed in jeans and a T-shirt, I lie down beside her, cover us with a comforter, pull her into my arms, and fall asleep.

CHAPTER NINE

Juliet

Although we never have an actual conversation about my moving into Cody's bedroom and sharing it with him, it just happens.

Like falling asleep.

Like breathing.

Like blinking.

Little by little over the next two weeks, the furniture from my room ends up in his. My fresh sheets and brand-new comforter now cover his aqua-painted bed. The little shelf that holds my clothes sits beside his bureau, and the nightstand and lamp from my room now rest on my side of Cody's bed. Gone is his nasty, old, vomit-yellow chair, exchanged for my pretty gingham bean bag and fuzzy throw blanket. Even his old carpet makes its way to the dump and my sage green carpet from upstairs warms our feet in the mornings.

And this morning when I open my eyes?

He's roped the room with the Christmas lights and sage-green ribbon while I was asleep.

How he pulled that off in the middle of the night, I'll never know, but in its own way, it's so achingly romantic, it almost makes me cry.

The only things that have stayed upstairs are my air mattress, desk, laptop, and heater. When I need to work, as I do now, the loft is still my office.

It shows Cody's thoughtfulness that while he stealthily relocated me to his bedroom, he left some of what I needed behind for privacy and work. It makes me—*I don't know. Yes, I do*—it makes me like him so much that *like* doesn't feel like the right word anymore. No man has ever anticipated my needs so keenly or made my comfort such a priority. Cody shows his affection for me in action, in attention, and I value it more than every flowery word ever spoken.

Sometimes, when I wake up naked beside him, with his dark room smelling of our lovemaking, I'm filled with a sensation so strong, so absolute, I almost feel like I'm a part of him. And I wonder if human beings can forge a bond so intimate, so intense, so fierce that even when your bodies aren't physically joined together, your heart still beats in *his* chest, and his breath is the air that fills *your* lungs.

My feelings for him have grown in the same way that his bedroom has become mine. Organically, without permission or trial, my affection for him deepens day by day until I fear a time will come that I won't be able to remember when it didn't exist.

It will just…be.

Like blinking.

Like breathing.

Like falling asleep beside him or in his arms.

I won't just be Juliet Sanderson anymore. I'll be *Cody's* Juliet, and I think maybe I'll want to die if I ever have to be less than that.

From the window over my desk, I watch Cody open the kennel gate for all eighteen dogs after two hours of free play in the pasture. With their tails high and wagging, each dog enters the fenced area without hesitation. They aren't leashed or harnessed. They could bolt for the mountains at any time and only stop running when they so chose.

But they don't bolt. They don't run.

They come home to Cody, whom they love.

And they stay.

My email program chirps at me, demanding my attention, and I glance down at my laptop, clicking on Gmail to see who's looking for me.

Hmm. Wi-Fi must have been down for a while, because I have sixteen messages waiting for me. I delete twelve that are just spam and look at the remaining four. Two from Dr. Grant, one from my brother, and one from...*ugh*...Professor Steinbuck.

I click on Braydon's first, which is basically just a list of links to affordable flights on Expedia and Travelocity and an email urging me to come home at Thanksgiving. Sighing softly, I move it to my Braydon's Emails folder.

In my heart, I've decided that I want to stay here for Thanksgiving, and I think part of me is running down the clock so that the cost of leaving will be so prohibitive, I'll be forced to stay. I don't want to hurt my parents or brother, but I also can't bear to think of Cody all alone. The problem is, Cody hasn't asked me to stay. It's a topic I need to broach with him soon, but I don't want to come off as either mothering or clingy, so I've been dragging my feet.

I open the two emails from Sheila Grant, perusing them quickly. One is a confirmation that she received my notes from last week. The other asks me to clarify some points in the notes about the dogs' diet and care. I answer her questions, reminding myself to be more specific with my notes about details that will be hard to remember once I am back at school.

Finally, I open Glenn's email, taking a deep breath before I start reading.

Hi, Juliet:

I've been thinking about you a lot lately and wondering how you're getting on in Nome. According to Sheila Grant, you're working with a very junior musher, Cody Garrison, who has yet to successfully race in the Yukon Quest or the Iditarod.

I have reached out to some of my contacts in the area on your behalf, and found a placement for you with Jacques Favreau, a Quebecois musher who recently relocated to Kotzebue, Alaska, which is located to the northwest of Nome.

Jacques has twice won the Défi Taïga 200, he placed second in the Ivakkak last year, eighth in the Yukon Quest and tenth in the Iditarod. You should be able to relocate to Kotzebue just in time for the first heavy snowfall. With a kennel of twenty-six racing dogs, you will be kept busy working with him and his animals for the remainder of your fellowship.

I'm sure you will agree with me (and Sheila, with whom I took the liberty of speaking about this terrific opportunity) that staying with Jacques would be a major improvement in your learning experience, and I hope this gesture will—in some small way—make amends for the way we parted. Please let me know when Jacques may expect you in Kotzebue.

I didn't expect to miss you quite as much as I do, Juliet.

Be well and with much affection,

Glenn

I finish reading and slam my laptop closed, jumping up from my desk seat and eyeing the computer like a snake.

"How dare you!" I growl, clenching my jaw with fury.

I plop down on my air mattress, then lie back, staring up at the ceiling, my body practically shaking with anger.

What right does Stein*fuck* have to walk back into my life and call the shots? And fucking Sheila? She approved this switch-up without even mentioning it to me? No. *Fucking…no.* I'm not going anywhere. Absolutely not.

Crossing back over to my desk, I hit Reply, and start writing a message to Stein*fuck*, cc'ing Dr. Grant.

Dear Professor Steinbuck:

Thank you for your interest in my fellowship, but I am having an excellent experience with Cody Garrison, who has allowed me unfettered access to his dogs, and is, in fact, training me to race the Qimmiq, instead of just allowing me to observe his interactions with the eighteen dogs in his care. It's been a very hands-on experience so far, and as Dr. Grant can share with you, I have already submitted over a hundred pages of notes that act as the basis for this dissertation. As generous as it is, your offer to work with Jacques Favreau comes a bit too late. I am sure you can appreciate that after six weeks of research and bonding with Mr. Garrison's animals, I'm not anxious to start over.

Mr. Garrison plans to race in the Iditarod, which means that the rigors of his training schedule should be equal to that of Favreau, and with the first snowfall imminent, moving to a different location in Alaska feels illogical.

Thank you, again, for your kind words and thoughtful suggestions.

Juliet Sanderson

I read through what I've written before pressing Send, satisfied that I've used as professional a tone as possible, then close my laptop.

This is the second time that Glenn's reached out to me in six weeks, and I really don't get it. I clearly didn't mean anything to him. He was sleeping around. So why all of this attention now? Just trying to prove to me that he's a great professor? I never disputed that fact. I just think he's a shitty human being.

All of this makes me long for Silvia. *(I mean, it's not like I can talk to Cody about the professor I was banging.)* So I unplug my phone from its charger and open a text box to Sil.

JULIET:

Hey, stranger. Miss me yet?

SILVIA:

JULIET! OMG! Long time, no talk! Yes, I miss you! Give me an update!! I haven't heard from you in weeks!

JULIET:

Well…things took a turn with the guy. The musher. Cody.

SILVIA:

I knew it! I knew it! I knew it! OMG! You're in love, aren't you?!

JULIET:

Love is a strong word, Sil. We're…together.

SILVIA:

Is he AMAZING in bed?

JULIET:

Yes.

SILVIA:

OMG OMG OMG OMG OMG! I knew it! I love this so hard! You're paving the way for me to find MY hot Alaskan man someday!

JULIET:

LOL. We'll see.

Hey, I heard from Steinfuck today. He's interfering in my project. He wanted me to leave here and go observe a different musher all the way across the state.

SILVIA:

I'm not surprised. Your guy is hot.

JULIET:

How would Steinfuck know that? And why would it matter?

SILVIA:

It's called the internet…and because you two used to fuck.

JULIET:

Okay. But he didn't want to be with me. Obviously.

SILVIA:

Did he say that? I don't remember him saying that.

JULIET:

Don't you remember? He was with that other girl, Sil.

SILVIA:

Right. I know, but that doesn't mean he didn't want to be with you too. He probably wanted to be with both of you. Alphas don't like to choose, J, and they

certainly don't like to be rejected. They want to mate with WHO they want WHEN they want. You know that. In fact, by walking away from him, you probably triggered some sort of biological chase instinct in him.

Ugh.

She's right.

If Glenn sees himself as an alpha male, he wants to fuck all the bitches he can. And as the one bitch he cannot have anymore, I've instigated a stalking instinct in Glenn. He wants what he can't have. That's why he can't stop thinking about me. That's why he's meddling in my business. And the fact that my man is movie-actor-hot and ten years younger than Stein*fuck* is probably driving him nuts.

Well, too bad.

I don't want him. Not at all. Not even a little bit.

In fact, when I think back on the brief and tawdry sexcapade I shared with Glenn and compare it to what I'm sharing with Cody right now, the differences are so vast as to make my liaison with Glenn feel like a raindrop…while what I have with Cody feels more like an ocean.

JULIET:

You're exactly right! Thanks, Sil. I miss you! Talk soon?

SILVIA:

You bet! And while you're up there, do some recon for me! xo

Downstairs, I hear Cody come inside and turn on the sink, no doubt starting tonight's dinner routine, and I smile, plugging my phone back in and running downstairs, eager to help him in any way I can.

**

Cody

Thanksgiving.

It's all I can think about lately.

That, for four days, Juliet won't be barefoot in the kitchen making breakfast,

won't be sitting next to me in the golf cart or behind me in the sled while we run the dogs,

won't wash her hair in my shower with her vanilla shampoo,

won't fall asleep reading on the couch and need to be carried to bed,

won't reach for me in the night, peppering my lips with kisses, or guiding me into the willing warmth of her body,

won't be the last thing my eyes see when I fall asleep at night or the first when I wake up in the morning,

won't be…here.

And it *hurts*, which is crazy, because I've only known her for six weeks.

But that's all the time it took for me to fall in love with her: six weeks…to fall totally and completely in love.

I had no idea I was capable for feeling this much…for anyone. And now that I know, I can't decide if it's a blessing or a curse because losing her is inevitable, but I don't know how I will survive it.

When I lost my fingers, the doctor told me that once in a while, I might still feel them, and they might cause me pain. He called it "phantom pain," and I'm reminded of that now: the pain of something you once had that's now gone.

One day soon, I will reach for Juliet only to discover that she's no longer there, and I will figure out how to deal with that eventuality, but fuck me, but I cannot *bear* to lose any days between then and now.

I don't care if it's pushy or not: I need to know her plans. And maybe more important, I need her to know that I want her to stay.

After the dogs have been fed and our dinner dishes have been washed, I look for her in our room, only to realize she's in the shower. I can hear John Denver singing "Annie's Song" through the wall, and I sit down on the bed for a second, intending to wait for her. I'll bring up Thanksgiving as soon as she's finished...but then I imagine her in the shower, her skin slick from warm water and soap, and another plan quickly takes shape.

When I open the curtain, standing before her in my birthday suit, with a massive erection, I half expect her to tell me to get lost, but she grins at me, giggling as she leans back to get the suds out of her long hair.

"You coming...in?" she asks.

"I was thinking about it," I say, my lips twitching because I love it when she's a little sassy. It turns me on like a lightbulb.

"Not sure there's room for the three of us," she says,

glancing meaningfully at my cock before leaning her head back again.

She knows full and well that leaning back shoves her breasts in my face, and I waste no time reaching for them as I step inside the steamy stall with her. They're slick as wet silk, her skin smooth and pink from the hot water. I lean forward and take one nipple between my lips, puckering around it before I let it go. Her breathing and heart rate speed up—I can tell by the way her chest rises and lowers, by the way the heartbeat in her neck suddenly beckons me like a beacon. With my left hand, I fondle her other breast while my lips touch down on her throat, licking that pulse point so slowly, I can feel her heartbeat on my tongue.

Just then, the song changes and John Denver intones, *"It's by far the hardest thing I've ever done...to be so in love with you, so alone..."*

I close my eyes, pulling her into my arms and holding her tightly against my body. She winds her arms around my neck, letting them hang loose and limp over my shoulders. And suddenly, what started off as sexy shower time, has turned into us slow dancing under a gentle spray of warm water.

"Don't leave," I hear myself whisper close to her ear.

"What?" she murmurs.

"Stay here for Thanksgiving," I say. "I know—"

"Cody—"

"—it probably doesn't sound like much fun, but I'll...I can make it better, um, fun. We could have Jonas and Rita over, or—"

"Cody—"

"Before you say no, just…just think about it. I'll do—I mean, I'm an okay cook, right? I'll do all the cooking and you can just—"

"Cody!"

She leans back, looking up at me, her arms still draped around my neck, though she clasps her hands together and her eyes flare like she means business.

"What?" I ask.

There are droplets of water sticking to her eyelashes like diamond dust, and my heart clutches because she's so beautiful and I can offer her so little. Surely, she's about to tell me that she's already made plans to go hom—

"I'd love to stay," she says.

I'm so surprised, I blink at her, my lips parting and my chest tightening with a deep sob I never felt coming. I cough to cover it, pulling her back into my arms because if I look into her sweet, kind eyes, it'll be too much.

"You're…staying?" I ask.

"Yeah. I mean, I want to," she says, "if it's okay with you, which I guess…"

"It is."

She takes a deep breath, pressing her lips to my shoulder for a second before laying her cheek on my shower-soaked skin.

"My brother sent me an email with all these flights this morning, but I couldn't even write back. It felt…I mean, the thought of leaving felt…"

I stroke her back because if her feelings for me are

anything like mine for her, I know exactly how it felt. "Awful."

"Awful," she agrees in a soft and small voice. "I don't know what's happening between us. I only know that I think about you all the time. I love being here with you, learning from you…I'm not saying this right…"

"You're doing great, beautiful."

"I want to stay," she says, with a soft, almost surprised, laugh. "So I guess I will."

She leans up to look at me, her eyes lingering on my lips. I know what she wants. I want the same thing. Reaching behind her, I turn off the water, then take her hand, leading her out of the shower.

Grabbing a towel from the shelf beside the shower, I wrap her up, rubbing her arms before giving her a light smack on the bottom. "I'll meet you in bed."

"Don't be long," she orders me, slipping out the door as I grab a second towel for myself.

Because I don't want to let my woman down, I dry myself quickly, rolling on a little deodorant and brushing my teeth for good measure.

When I walk naked into our bedroom, she's turned on the Christmas lights only, and the room is filled with a warm glow. Juliet lies in the middle of the bed on her side, her hair towel-dried and wavy, her skin milky and smooth in the dim light.

"How is this possible?" I ask, lying down on my back beside her.

"*This?*"

"You and me."

"Oh," she says, dropping her index finger on my chest to trace hearts on my skin. "Us."

"*Us*. It should be impossible."

"It's not."

"A beautiful, young goddess like you. A broken, old veteran like me—"

"With a face like a movie star," she interjects, placing a sweet kiss inside one of the hearts she's drawn.

"You're ten years younger than I am," I say.

"Yep," she says. "When you got your driver's license, I was in first grade."

"Does that bother you?"

"My last boyfriend was in his forties, so…no."

I didn't know this. I don't like it, because I irrationally hate any man who's ever been intimate with her. But some stupid part of me is also comforted by it because it means that liking older guys is a pattern for her, not some weird new experiment that she's trying out for the first time.

"Why'd you break up with him?"

She looks at me for a second, about to say something, then goes back to drawing. "*He* broke it off."

"Right before they hauled him away to an insane asylum?"

She snorts with laughter and the sound is so awesome, I reach for her under the arms, sliding her body onto my chest. I can feel the tight points of her nipples against my pecs, and it makes me suck in a breath as my cock, which never really softened much in the shower, thickens and hardens.

Her blue eyes lock onto my green as she sits up, grasping onto the base of my erection. Positioning herself over it, she lowers her body slowly, never taking her eyes away from mine, and fuck if it's not the most intense thing I've ever experienced.

"Juliet…" I say, gasping softly as she sheaths me to the balls. "I'm…I'm falling for you."

She leans forward, placing her palms flat on my chest. "I know."

"Hard," I say.

"I know," she says again, dropping her lips to mine as I reach for her hips, so I can guide her movements.

I pull her forward, impaling her, then push her back, before sliding her close again. After a few minutes of my being in control, however, her hands land on mine when I'm in deep. She stays still, with my cock fully inside of her, and squeezes the walls of her pussy around me. I gasp, feeling my balls, swollen with cum, tighten. While we're connected as intimately as humanly possible, she takes my scarred, mangled hands and places them over her perfect breasts, then covers them with her own.

And that's when I realize why it's been so easy to fall in love with this woman.

Because she doesn't shrink back from the ugly parts of me.

Because she embraces all of me—the good parts, the ugly parts, and everything in between.

Still holding my hands against her skin, she looks into

my eyes.

"I'm falling for you too," she says softly, her eyes glistening with emotion.

Jackknifing into a sitting position, I wrap my arms around her, pulling her tightly against my chest. She wraps her legs around my waist, and I thrust up into the sweet heaven of her body once…twice…three times.

Her forehead falls on my shoulder, as she goes rigid, then slack, her muscles vibrating against my cock. It only takes one more deep thrust for me to climax with her, coming in surges of hot cum that baptize the sacred shrine where I worship.

Holding each other tightly, we ride out our shared bliss together: two unlikely halves of a perfect whole, two wandering souls bound by new love.

CHAPTER TEN

Juliet

The smell of roasting turkey basted with butter wakes me up…and if there's a better alarm clock in the entire world, I have yet to figure out what it is.

At home, my mother and father are no doubt bustling around the kitchen, getting everything ready for my extended family, who'll be arriving any minute. The Macy's Thanksgiving Day Parade, just about to end now, will be showing on every TV, and Braydon will be helping set the table with his girlfriend, Kristy.

My family was disappointed in my decision to stay in Nome for Thanksgiving, but I agreed to come home for Christmas, which softened the blow. I have the same feelings about leaving Cody at Christmas as I had about leaving him at Thanksgiving, but maybe—just maybe—I can persuade him to come home with me. No, I don't know who'd look after the dogs, and no, I don't know if a man who hasn't left Alaska in over a decade would even consider coming to Montana for a few days, but I'll wait for the right moment, cross my fingers, and hope for the best.

The light filtering in through the windows tells me it's much later than usual, and I look at my phone to see that it's almost ten o'clock. Cody let me sleep in, which means he's not only preparing Thanksgiving dinner for us and our guests, Jonas, Rita, and their son, Mitchell, but he also took care of the dogs' breakfast on his own.

Stretching my arms over my head, I think about Cody in broader terms, further down the road of life—as a husband and a father. He'll be the best, I decide, feeling envious of the woman he marries someday. He'll be hands-on and involved, grateful for the people he loves and eager to make them happy. Will she even realize how lucky she is? How lucky her children are? Will she know that of all the men in the world she could have married, that she got a man who will intentionally and faithfully love her longer and harder and better than most other men would even be willing to try?

I sigh, sitting up and swinging my legs off the side of the bed.

I hate her, I think.

I hate her so much for the amazing future she's going to have with him.

I'll be a vet in Missoula, working with my dad and brother. I'll probably end up marrying one of Braydon's friends, who, honestly, are all very nice guys.

But none of them is Cody, whispers my heart.

Maybe not, I think. But we'll buy a beautiful house in a nice neighborhood, with a green lawn and landscaped gardens. We'll have two or three kids, that play little league or take ballet lessons, who will grow up with lots of family nearby.

It'll be a good life, I tell myself. *The sort of life you always dreamed of, Juliet.*

I look around Cody's bedroom—at the mostly bare walls and mismatched furniture. Outside it's gray and cold, and after only two snowfalls, the icy winter hasn't even set in yet. He's chosen to live at the edge of the world. And truly, I have loved being here with him for a few months. But forever?

I sigh.

I can't picture it. I don't think Nome would make me happy long-term…even if it included Cody.

But today isn't a day for such worries, I think, standing up and shrugging into my bathrobe. Today is a day for gratitude.

After all, it's Thanksgiving, and I'm spending it with the man I adore.

***

"So Mitchy sees that bear comin' at him, and he freezes," says Rita, telling a story at the Thanksgiving table, "and it's all Jonas can do to get the shotgun aimed in time, but hell if he don't. Got that grizzly between the eyes. Bear went down. Son was spared. An' I got a nice, new rug."

Mitchell Beaudoin clears his throat, then rolls his eyes at me with embarrassment. As the youngest guest at our table, he's been getting a little hazing by his parents, and while it's good-natured, I'm sensing he's had enough.

"Mitch," I say, "your parents said you're in college?"

"Yep," he answers, taking another serving of Cody's stuffing. "Junior year. I go to the University of Alaska, Southeast."

"Where's that?"

"Juneau."

"You like it there?"

He grins at me, and it's impossible not to smile back. With dark hair like his mother and light eyes like his father, he's very good-looking and quite charming.

"It's a lot warmer down there," he says. "And there's a lot more to do."

"City life," says Rita, taking a sip of the wine they brought. "I don't know why anyone would prefer it there to here."

"*Aana!*" cries Mitchell, using the Yupik word for mom. "You can't be serious!"

"Oh, I'm serious, all right," she says. "Juneau's a big place. Got ten times as many people there as here."

"Sure does," agrees her son. "Plus, it's warmer, easier to get things, and a lot more interesting. There's theaters and festivals, all those government buildings with people comin' and goin'—"

"You can keep 'em," says Rita, waving her hand dismissively.

"—lots of good hiking, but there's also businesses and opportunity. Museums. More places to see, more people to know."

"If it's so great," grumbles his mother, "then why come home at all?"

"Because I love you and Pop," he says, winking at her. "Can't get rid of me that easy, *Aana*."

She beams back at him, shaking her head like she disapproves, but pleased as punch for all to see.

Mitchell turns to me. "Pop tells me you're studying to be a vet?"

I nod. "Yep. I'm in my final year at the University of Minnesota."

"You from there? Minnesota?"

"Nope. Montana."

"Race to the Sky country," he says, which surprises me. This entire group of people identifies parts of the world based on which sled dog competitions take place there, Mitchell included.

"Do you race?" I ask him.

"Ma and Cody tried to teach me when I was a kid. Didn't take."

I glance across the table at Cody, who stares at Mitchell with an inscrutable expression, and suddenly I realize he's been a little quiet since the Beaudoins arrived. I wonder what's up with him. Rita and Jonas usually put him in good spirits. He's comfortable with them.

"Cody's a great teacher," I tell Mitch, flicking my eyes at Cody, only to find him staring down at his plate, his eyebrows furrowed together. I turn back to Mitch. "We're racing the Qimmiq together—everything I know, I've learned from him."

"When do you go back to college?" asks Mitch, changing the subject.

"January."

"Yeah. Me too. We start up again on the twenty-first."

"Same here. I guess that's pretty standard at American universities."

161

"You know," says Mitch, giving me a teasing smile, "UAS has an amazing marine mammal research program. If you ever decide to switch from land animals to sea mammals, I'd be happy to show you around the campus."

"After almost eight years in school, I think I'm ready for a break," I tell him with a chuckle.

Cody clears his throat. "You got a girlfriend down there in Juneau, Mitch?"

"Mitchy's too young for a girlfriend," teases Jonas.

"Pop, I'm almost twenty-one." He turns to me, cocking his head to the side with a flirtatious grin. "How old are you, Juliet? If you don't mind my asking."

"Twenty-four."

"You got a boyfriend?"

I slide my eyes from Mitch to Cody, who looks like a thunder cloud at the end of the table.

"In fact, I do," I say, winking at Cody.

"Wait…not *Cody*," says Mitch, looking back and forth between us.

"Why not?" asks Cody, while I say, "Yep," at the same time.

"But he's—"

"Mitchy," interrupts Rita. "How about you open that other bottle of wine we brought? I stuck it in the fridge."

"He's—"

"Mitchell, the wine," says Rita firmly.

"… twice your age," mumbles Mitch, standing up from the table and heading into the kitchen.

"No, he's not," I say softly, staring at Cody like we're

the only two people in the world. "He's just right."

Cody gives me a small, fake smile, but his face is drawn and troubled…and I hate it.

We have dessert in the living room, and after dinner, Mitch and Jonas give Cody a hand feeding the dogs while Rita helps me with the dishes. We stand at the sink together while she washes, and I dry and put away.

"Cody's a good cook," she says in her broad Alaskan accent.

"The best," I say. "We have a deal that I make breakfast and he makes dinner. I'm winning that bargain."

She nods. "He did a lot of planning when you said you were comin'. Got that room up there all spruced up for you."

"And you helped," I say, drying a mixing bowl, "which I appreciate, Rita."

"Uh-huh. You know, Cody…he cares for you."

"I care about him too."

"No," she says, looking at me. "I don't mean it like that. I mean…Cody's falling in love with you."

Heretofore, Cody's only told me that he was "falling" for me, which is a far more casual expression of feeling. There hasn't been any mention of love yet, and frankly, with a solid end-date to our relationship on the horizon, it would be best if he didn't. It'll only make things harder when I have to go.

"I'm the only woman he's been around for a long time," I say, trying to downplay her words. "We're both infatuated. But—"

She places a soapy hand on my arm. "Cody's *falling in love* with you."

Her dark eyes seize my blue, and I am forced to feel the gravitas of her words.

Falling…in love.

It's different from caring about someone. It's even different from loving someone. *Falling in love* is actionable. It's intense and possessive. But it's also involuntary. You can be sensible about caring or loving, but it's impossible to maintain any perspective or much logic as you fall. It happens too fast—like all physical and emotional falls in nature—to be controlled. It's a wild thing, with an energy and forward momentum of its own.

Her gaze is too intense, so I slip my arm from her grasp and turn around, busying myself with wrapping some leftover pumpkin pie in plastic wrap.

"He hasn't said that." Not exactly, anyway.

"But you know it's true," she says, resuming her scrubbing.

Part of me—a primal part of my humanness, of my womanhood, that speaks nonverbally and understands instinctually—acknowledges that Rita is speaking the truth. But another part of me—the part interested in self-preservation, or in comfortable logic—would prefer other, less incendiary, less frightening, terminology.

"I only know what he tells me. And he told me he's 'falling' for me." I laugh awkwardly. "No mention of love."

Rita places a rinsed platter in the drying rack and looks at me. "Okay. If you say so."

Her eyes are calling me out on bullshit. Yeah, she's said her piece and she's not going to pursue it, but she also believes that Cody's falling in love with me, and the sheer force of her conviction forces me to acknowledge that it's true.

"Cody's been through a lot," she says. "Don't hurt him."

"I...I won't," I say, though my words, like the good intentions behind them, feel flimsy. I already know that leaving Cody in January is going to hurt *me*. I can only imagine how much it's going to hurt him too.

***

Cody

I watch the way Mitch ladles out the food for my dogs—it's so effortless for him with ten perfect fingers and a body fourteen years younger than mine. His movements are fluid, not jerky. There are no spills. He lifts each bowl with the thumb and four fingers of his left hand, then fills the ladle, steadying it mostly with his thumb and index finger like a pencil and effortlessly dumping the contents neatly into each bowl.

I'm mesmerized watching him do such simple movements that I once took for granted.

I'm...jealous.

Hell, I've been jealous for hours, I think, turning away from Mitch to check on Salem's front left paw. I pulled a thorn out of it two days ago and she's still favoring the right. Maybe I didn't get it all.

"Hey, Pop!" Mitch shouts toward the grub shack. "You almost ready with the leftovers? Got three dogs left!"

"Coming, son!"

Mitch is almost twenty-one, the same age I was when I lost my fingers.

He's also four years younger than Juliet to my ten older.

How can I possibly compete with someone like him?

I'm just an old guy, his parents' friend…*twice your age*.

I saw the way he looked at her—the way his handsome face lit up and his green eyes twinkled. She likes green eyes. Wouldn't she like them all the better in the face of a man who has all ten fingers, only a few years younger than she, with none of the baggage I have?

Mitch had a loving, stable childhood with Jonas and Rita. He's studying marine biology at college, a perfect complement to Juliet's veterinary studies. He's got his whole life ahead of him.

Me? The best years of my life are long gone. I had a shitty childhood and no formal education. I served the Marines in on-the-ground logistics, which didn't shield me from seeing the horrors of combat or prevent me from retiring with a permanent, and grotesque, disability.

While Mitch is down there in Juneau embracing city-life—mixing it up with different people, and experiencing life to the fullest—I choose to stay about as far away from civilization as possible, hidden away in a tiny town where I can live my life under the radar, where my hands in snow gloves can go, mostly, unnoticed.

But I can't expect someone as vibrant and young as

Juliet to stay hidden up here with me…not that she'd want to…not that I'd ask. I care about her too much to ever ask her to hide her light from a world that deserves the brightness of her beauty.

I should stop loving her.

(I wish to God I could.)

"Hey! How's Salem's foot?" I look up to see her standing over me, and my whole body reacts—she's the lodestone to my iron, and all I want to do is fuse myself to her forever. "She still favoring the right?"

"Looks that way."

"Cody, we got 'em all fed," says Jonas, approaching us with Mitch by his side. "Mitchy, go tell your *aana* we gotta get going. I got two cats and a dog at my office that need to be looked in on before we can head home for the night."

I offer my hand to Jonas, grateful for my friend. "Thanks for coming."

"Thanks for having us," he says. "You roast a mean turkey." He turns to Juliet. "Good to see you again, too."

She leans in to hug Jonas. "You too."

Rita and Mitch approach us from the house, bundled up to go home.

"Thanks for Thanksgiving, Cody," says Rita. "I left you the wine and the rest of the apple pie."

"Thanks," I say, letting her cup my cheeks over the chain link of the kennel fence.

"You be good now," she says. Her eyes shift to Juliet. "And you remember what I said."

"Oh. I, um…" Juliet clears her throat. "I will."

Mitch lets himself back into the kennel area to hug Juliet. "It was great meeting you. Offer to visit me in Juneau stands. Anytime."

Every muscle in my body clenches, but I don't move.

"I'll keep it in mind." Juliet chuckles, patting his back before stepping out of his arms. "You're a terrible flirt, Mitch."

"Yeah, well…can't blame a guy for trying." He shrugs, giving me a sheepish look as he backs up through the gate to join his parents. "Thanks for dinner, Cody."

"Get back to Juneau safe," I say, putting an arm around Juliet and pulling her against my side in lieu of pissing on her leg.

"Well," says Juliet, after we've waved good-bye, "that was…*interesting*."

"What did Rita say to you?"

"Just girl talk."

"Seemed important."

She gives me a look that reads: *It's none of your business*, so I let it go.

"Let's bring Salem in tonight," I say, crouching down to unhook her collar from the stake next to her doghouse. "I want a better look at that paw."

I pick up the husky, holding her close to my chest as Juliet opens the kennel gate and the front door to the house. She's quiet and, I suspect, upset about something, but fuck and hell, I'm a little upset too. Mitch flirted with her all night, and she seemed fine with it. Not to mention, being around Mitch just confirmed what I already knew: that Juliet deserves so much more than me. That no matter how much we're enjoying each other now, *now* has a sell-by date, and it's less than two months away.

I settle Salem on the green rug in the bedroom, near the stove, and watch as Vi approaches the younger dog cautiously. They sniff each other, Salem jumping up for a second to smell and be smelled, but after deciding neither is a threat to the other, or maybe just reintroducing their brains to one another's scent, they curl up butt to butt and close their eyes.

Juliet's taken off her coat and boots by the time I turn around to find her sitting on the edge of the bed. I ignore her as I head to the hallway closet to find tweezers and wet a washcloth in the bathroom. I feel a fight brewing between us, and frankly, I'm not sure how I feel about it. Part of me wants to avoid it, and part of me is spoiling for it.

Unfortunately, however, I'm going to need her help first. Of the many things I've taught myself how to do with five fingers, using tweezers is almost impossible. I can pinch things between the thumb and pinky of my right hand, but it's clumsy at best. I don't want to hurt Salem, and I suspect the little piece of thorn bothering her is in deep.

"I think she's got some of that thorn still stuck in her paw," I tell Juliet, placing the tweezers on her knee and holding the hot washcloth in my hand.

"Hmm." She kneels down on the floor, petting Salem gently for a second before turning over her foot. "Can you use my phone as a flashlight?"

I grab her phone from the bedside table, noticing the

cache of waiting messages from her friends and family, which makes me feel even worse about today. She missed out on Thanksgiving with her friends and family…for what? For dinner with a cranky old man and his measly group of friends.

She hunches closer to Salem, gently explaining to my dog what she's doing. "I just want to take a look, pretty girl. I think I can help."

I hold the light steady for her—the least I can do—as she inspects the soft, furry spots between Salem's pads.

"Yep," she says when Salem whimpers. "It's swollen and painful. Here it is."

As she works on squeezing the area to ease the thorn base out, alternating use of her fingers and wiping off the increasingly bloody paw with the hot cloth, I decide it's the right time for us to chat.

So with my usual grace, I blurt out: "You should be with someone like Mitch."

Her neck snaps up and Salem half whimpers, half snarls because her finger slips.

"Are you seriously going to do this while I'm doctoring an injured animal?"

"I'm just saying…"

She soothes Salem with some sweet words, then goes back to what she was doing.

"I don't want to be with Mitch," she says softly, concentrating on her patient. "I get it that he and I are closer in age than you and I, but emotionally, he's about a decade younger than I am."

"He's got his whole life ahead of him," I say.

She raises her eyes to mine, her expression pissed. "Give me the tweezers. It's coming to a head."

I hand them to her and press on with my thoughts. "He's—"

"If you say one more word about Mitchell Beaudoin and I getting together, I will throw these tweezers in your face, walk to town, and stay overnight at a hotel."

"Good luck finding a room over a holiday weekend."

"I'll find one," she tells me, somehow keeping her voice even, though I know I'm making her mad.

"I'm sure there are a lot of nice, young guys at your college."

"I'm sure there are."

"And you'd be better off with one of them."

"Believe me," she says without looking up, "you're acting like such a jerk right now, they're all looking pretty good."

"I'm not trying to be a jerk," I tell her. "I'm trying to tell you that we shouldn't be together...that I'm not good enough for you. I'm too old. I'm too broken. I'm too much of a mess. You could do a lot better than—"

"Got it!" she says, holding up the tweezers in victory. There, clasped between the tiny points, is a sizeable piece of thorn. She picks up the washcloth and rubs it over Salem's foot. "You'll feel better now, I promise."

"You, uh," I say, holding her phone out to her. "You have a lot of messages."

She takes the phone from my hand and throws it up on

the bed without looking at it, holding my eyes all the while. And damn if I don't start feeling like the younger one between us because she looks like an angry schoolteacher, about to rap my knuckles for doing something wrong.

"Why do you think I stayed here for Thanksgiving?" she demands.

I shrug. "You felt sorry for me?"

"Honestly? Yes. Maybe a little. Spending a holiday all alone sucks." She cocks her head to the side. "But sympathy was…hmm…less than ten percent of my decision. What's the *main reason* I stayed?"

I stare at her, waiting for her to say more.

"What the hell do you think this is?" she cries.

"This…*what*?"

"This…*us*!" she yells.

Viola stands up, coming to sit beside me, and Salem whimpers, looking back and forth between us.

"I don't know what the future holds!" she shouts. "I don't know what will happen when I leave here in January! But I don't care if you're thirty-four. I don't care if you're *fifty*-four. My heart has already decided what it wants. Whatever you are, whoever you are, *you're what I want!* I don't want Mitch Beaudoin, you dumbass! *I'm in love with you!*"

I sit there on the carpet, across from her, and watch her face as her mouth drops open. I'm fairly certain that she didn't mean to say that last part because she blinks at me, then clenches her jaw tight and stares down at her lap.

"And now you're *also* the jerk that made me say too much before I was ready," she murmurs, her voice small and upset.

I'm in love with you!

I reach for her hands with mine, letting her lace her fingers through mine where she can, and swallowing over the lump in my throat.

In love with...*me*. It can't be. It's not possible.

"You're...in love with m-me?" my voice breaks on the whispered words.

"Yeah," she says, staring down at our hands. "I am."

I squeeze her hands in mine, and speak softly, my words prayerlike and reverent. "I never dared to hope that someone like you could fall in love with someone like me."

"Sorry." She finally looks up at me, her eyes glassy. "I couldn't help it."

My eyes flood with tears, but I'm somehow able to blink them back. She is holding my hands with hers—*my hands!*—and she's...in love with me.

"I'm in love with you too," I tell her.

She sniffles. "I know. Rita told me."

"I never told Rita!"

"You didn't have to," she says, a little smile finally brightening her face.

"It's that obvious?"

"I guess it is." Suddenly, she frowns. "So please stop saying that I should be with someone else, because it's like a thorn in my paw. Or a knife in my heart. It hurts me, Cody. I only want to be with you."

"I promise," I say. "I won't say anything like that again."

"You can trust this," she says.

This? Our feelings? Yes. Okay. I will trust that what we feel is real.

But the future? As she said earlier, she has no idea what will happen when she leaves in January, and neither do I. But if I worry about the *terrible-then*, I'll miss out on the *spectacular-now*.

"I trust it," I tell her, standing up and pulling her to her feet.

We undress quickly and fall in to bed, but then, while the dogs sleep soundly in front of the fire, we love each other slowly, all night long, our bodies tangled together until the dawn.

CHAPTER ELEVEN

Juliet

"Juliet! You *can't* let Gus call the shots!" yells Cody from behind me. "She's not listening to you! You're going to get the dogs, or—God forbid—yourself killed!"

Since Thanksgiving, we've had six major snowfalls, and Cody and I have been racing in sleds over snow for two weeks now. A clear day like today means a five-hour, fifty-mile run under blue skies with bright sun. It's cold as hell, but I've never experienced anything as unique and exhilarating as sled dog racing.

That said, today was terrifying, and Cody is right.

As much as I love Augusta, and as much as I've championed her, she's not working out as a lead dog. She's ignoring my commands and gets easily distracted by new sights and smells.

Today, while I was telling the team to turn right, she insisted on going left. Why? I discovered her reason about two minutes later when we happened upon a fourteen-point bull elk, who was not at all pleased to have eight dogs suddenly yapping at him.

He "bugled" angrily—a unique sound halfway between a scream and wail that reminded me a little of what a whale call might sound like out of water—leaning down to show his antlers to the dogs and edging forward like he might charge.

I screamed for Cheyenne and Augusta to back up, but Augusta kept urging them forward into a confrontation only curtailed when Cody caught up with us. Blocking our path, he fired his shotgun twice into the air, which, thank God, scared the elk, who ran back into the woods. But even then, Augusta tried to pursue him, which meant that my team got tangled up with his and had to be unraveled and straightened out before we could all head home.

It was a dangerous and awful experience and forced me to recognize what Cody knew all along: Augusta isn't cut out to be a lead dog. She needs to be demoted to team dog, for now.

I pull into the snowy area beside the kennel, exhausted after five hours of sledding and the elk encounter, and look over my shoulder at Cody.

"I know," I say, sliding my ski goggles to my forehead. "I know."

"Whoa, boys! Whoa! Whoaaaa."

Cody's team stops beside mine, and he swipes at his nose with a gloved hand, shaking his head. "She can't—"

"I know!" I say again, leaning down to begin the arduous process of unharnessing the dogs. "She can't be lead dog."

"I'm sorry," he says, putting his hands on his hips. "But you scared the hell out of me back there."

I unhook Cheyenne and August first, opening the kennel yard for them and watching them trot over to their houses to wait for a snack.

"I scared the hell out of myself," I tell him, unlatching Topeka, Juneau, Helena, Salem, Olympia, and Phoenix. I still need to take their harnesses off, but at least they aren't attached to each other and the sled anymore. "I'm going to get them food."

I head over to the grub shack, scooping up eight pieces of semithawed frozen meat strips. The dogs are howling by the time I enter the kennel, and I give each her snack, telling them all what a good job they did before heading back to my sled.

It takes Cody about five times as long to unlatch his dogs, so I help him, getting his two swing dogs, two team dogs, and two wheel dogs unlatched in the same time it takes him to free his leads, Dover and Boston. He herds them all into the kennel area, then grabs snacks for them too.

I remove the racing harnesses from all the dogs and hang up the equipment on pegs in the shipping container while Cody disassembles the sleds and pulls them inside. Once the dogs and sleds are taken care of, we take Denver and Concord, the two male dogs that didn't race today, into the paddock for some exercise, and lean on the split-level fence side by side.

"What are you going to do?" Cody asks me.

"I don't know."

"I think you should consider letting Chey lead alone."

"A seven-dog team?" I ask.

"She's the only one willing and ready. I don't have a second female trained to be lead. Closest in temperament is

Salem, I think, but she's too young." He shrugs. "Might be I just don't have a second female lead."

I know what he means. A good deal of the job a dog can handle is based on his or her inherent nature. Olympia and Phoenix, for instance, are great swing dogs. They're eager and willing to follow all of Cheyenne's instructions, enforcing her rule over the team. And Helena, the largest female of the pack, is a perfect wheel dog, using her muscle to carry out my turns and signals from close to the sled.

"I don't see another leader," I say.

"There isn't one," he agrees. "Let's try solo lead tomorrow."

"Who do we cut?" I ask.

"Topeka," he suggests, watching Denver chase Concord with unrestrained glee. "You need Gus for her strength. Make her a team dog next to Juneau, behind Phoenix and in front of Helena. They'll keep her in line."

I look up at him and grin. "Do you know how good you are at this?"

"Yeah?"

"Oh, yeah," I say, reaching up to cup his cheek with my mittened hand.

Since the snow started in earnest, we've been racing for hours a day, and dog meals have become a bigger deal since we've added another pot to each feeding, giving them the calories they need.

Still working up our stamina, Cody and I are wiped out after dinner every night and fall into bed utterly exhausted by eight. Though we sleep next to each other, we haven't had sex in days, and it feels like all we talk about lately is the dogs. It makes sense. The Qimmiq is in five weeks, and I still need a lot of practice to feel comfortable racing. But part of me misses the more carefree days of October and early November.

Christmas is only two weeks away, and I haven't asked Cody to join me yet. I understand the rigors of training now, and I feel certain he'll say no if I invite him, telling me it's bad enough that one of us is leaving and he can't leave too. And even though it makes sense, I'm just not sure I want to be rejected like that. But at the same time, I know I won't forgive myself if I don't take a chance and ask.

"You did really good today," he says. "You must have been scared."

"I was," I tell him. "And that *godawful* noise."

"The bugling? Yeah. It's intense."

"I'll say. I expected more of a roar and less of a shriek."

"It's surprising. That's for sure."

I clear my throat. "Hey, um…I wanted to ask you something."

His elbows still rest on the fence, but he turns away from the dogs, looking at me. "What's up?"

"So…you know how I'm going home for Christmas?" His grin fades. "December twenty-third to twenty-sixth. I know."

"Well, I was just—I mean, I was sort of hoping you'd consider…" I take a deep breath and exhale sharply. "…coming home with me."

He stares at me, expressionless, like it was the last thing

he expected me to say.

"You want me to come to Montana?"

I nod. "I want you to know you're welcome."

Inside, I cringe. That's not really what I mean. Yes, of course he's welcome, but I really *want* him to come. In a weird way, his coming to Montana would be a sign that a future—however unlikely—was possible between us. Part of me wants to say that, but part of me doesn't feel right pressuring him like that.

"Thanks," he says. "That's really nice."

"What do you think?"

"I don't know," he says. "I've got eighteen dogs here to look after. I can't just… leave them."

"Maybe Jonas and Rita could stop over to feed them and—"

"They need to be training," he says. "Jonas doesn't race, and while Rita grew up around sled dogs, using a three-dog team to go to town for groceries is night and day from racing."

"Will Mitch be home? Maybe he could…"

"You heard him," says Cody. "We tried to teach him to race. It didn't take."

"So…" I say, feeling much more emotional than I'd anticipated. "That's a no?"

"I'm sorry, darlin'," he says. "I just don't see how it would work."

The way he says *darlin'* for the first time curls my toes.

The context in which he says it makes me want to cry.

Because if he'll never leave Nome, I don't see how *we*

can work. I appreciate the fact that he's happy making this tiny town his whole world. But for me? There's a whole world out there waiting for me, and Nome isn't enough.

I take a deep breath, but when I exhale, it's shaky. "Okay."

"Hey...you're upset?"

"I just wish..."

We're interrupted by the sound of an arriving car or truck and the beep-beep of a horn in front of the house.

...*things were different.*

"Are you expecting anyone?" I ask.

He shakes his head. "Nope. You?"

"UPS maybe? I'll go check it out."

It's probably just the postman delivering something I forgot I ordered, but I'm a little relieved for a moment to myself. Fat tears crowd my eyes, and I swipe them away, embarrassed by them. Cody's never pretended to be anything aside from what he is: a retired Marine living in Nome and racing sled dogs. The choice to accept that life or reject it is up to me.

As I walk around the side of the house, I see a taxi waiting out front. The cabbie sees me and waves, backing up and pulling out of the driveway. I continue around the house to the front door where I see a man standing on Cody's front porch.

"Can I help you?"

And I swear to God, I almost faint when Glenn Steinbuck, dressed in jeans, boots and a brand-new parka, turns around to greet me.

"Jules!" he cries. "There you are!"

I stop dead in my tracks, staring at him, my mouth ajar, more shocked than I've ever been in my entire life.

"Wha…How did…What are you doing here, Glenn?"

He jumps off the porch and approaches me, his arms wide. "I came to see you, baby."

I take a step back, crossing my arms over my chest. "You flew from Minneapolis to Nome to…*see me*?"

"Not exactly. I was in Anchorage for an Iditarod Trail Committee meeting. Decided to catch a puddle jumper over to Kotzebue to see my old friend, Jacques, and I couldn't resist taking a commuter flight to check on you too."

"You didn't have to do that," I say.

"I know, baby," he says, reaching for my arms and pulling at them, forcing me to stop clenching them. "I wanted to."

He pulls me against his chest and hugs me, even though it should have been clear from my body language that I wasn't interested in being touched by him.

"Juliet? Who's here…?"

Cody's voice drifts off as he rounds the house to find me in Glenn's arms. I jump away from my erstwhile professor, pushing against his chest to make space between us.

"C-Cody…this is Glenn, um, Steinbuck. Glenn, this is Cody Garrison."

"Hey, there, Garrison. Good to meet you. I was Juliet's, um, professor…back in Minneapolis."

Glenn offers his hand to Cody, who looks at it for a

second, then shakes it. I watch Glenn's face carefully, catching the slight furrow of his brows when he shakes Cody's gloved hand. Cody pulls away quickly.

"Is this a surprise?" he asks, looking back and forth between me and Glenn.

"Yes," I say. *And not a good one.*

"I was just telling Jules…I was in Anchorage for an ITC meeting, then jumped a commuter flight to come say hello."

"Long way for a surprise hello," Cody observes, putting his hands on his hips.

"Well, Jules and I were…*special* friends."

The way he says it is so gross, I want to gag for ever letting him touch me.

Cody flicks his eyes to me. "*Jules*, huh?"

"Pet name," says Glenn, winking at me.

Enough is enough. "Glenn, I was pretty clear about staying here to train. I'm not interested in the opportunity in Kotzebue."

"Opportunity?" asks Cody.

"Yes," Glenn interjects. "A few weeks ago I told Jules about a musher in Kotzebue—maybe you've heard of him—Jacques Favreau?"

Cody doesn't give anything away, just stares stone-faced at Glenn.

Glenn grins, sensing an advantage he doesn't have. "Well, he offered to let Jules stay with him, observe, train, et cetera. No offense, Garrison, because this a cute operation you have here, but Favreau's kennel is…" He kisses his fingers like a chef. "…first class."

Sliding his eyes to me, Cody says, "You didn't mention this to me."

"Because I told Glenn I wasn't interested. Immediately. In no uncertain terms. I told him I wanted to stay here with you." I turn to Glenn. "Did we cross wires somewhere? I felt like I was clear in my email."

"Oh, you were," he says, smiling at me. "I just thought a personal visit could convince you to reconsider."

It's the sexy smile he used to flash at me from behind the podium at the front of the lecture hall—the one that used to get me turned on. Now? It just reminds me of a puddle-deep affair I'd just as well forget.

"I couldn't resist. I was so close," Glenn adds.

"Close? Anchorage?" asks Cody. "It's an hour and a half. By plane."

"Details," says Glenn. "When I want to be somewhere, I make it happen." He smirks at Cody, then skims his eyes to me. "I'm used to getting what I want."

Enough is enough…take two. I lift my chin, hoping my eyes are as icy as I feel. "Well, I'm afraid this visit isn't welcome, Glenn."

"Jules, give me a break," he says, looking uncertain for the first time since arriving. "I flew all the way here."

"I didn't ask you to do that," I say, taking a step closer to Cody.

Glenn looks at me, then Cody. Me, then Cody.

"Oh, shit," he says. He chuckles and it's a nasty, hollow sound. "You're fucking him."

Cody takes a step forward, nostrils flaring, and suddenly I'm reminded of the bull elk earlier today. I grab his arm and pull him back. "He's not worth it."

"*I'm* not worth it?" Glenn demands with another snarky laugh. "*I'm* a fully tenured college professor. A *doctor*. A respected animal *expert*. A valuable Iditarod *veterinarian*. Who's this guy? Some no-name musher who shakes hands like a girl!"

"Shut up, Glenn," I snarl, holding Cody's arm tighter.

I can feel the coiled anger he's throwing off like heat. Cody may not be able to make a perfect fist, but he's practically made of muscle. In a fight, Glenn's going down. No contest.

Alphas don't like to choose, J, and they certainly don't like to be rejected.

Sil's text slides through my mind, and it occurs to me that I'm watching a dick-measuring contest unfold here. I'm the female they've both mated with, and Glenn *thinks* he's the alpha, but he's about to get his ass beat by Cody, who *is* the alpha.

"Glenn, I'll call you a cab," I say. "You need to go. Now."

"Fuck you, Jules. You don't tell me what to do."

My hand on Cody's sleeve is no match for his fury.

He surges forward with a low growl and head-butts Glenn in the chest, knocking him to his back in the driveway. Leaping over to his rival, Cody kneels down, straddling Glenn's body with muscular thighs, then uses Glenn's face like a punching bag. Left, right. Left, right.

Lucky for Glenn, Cody's gloves act as shock absorbers and don't allow the full force of his anger to break every bone in Glenn's stupid face.

"Cody!" I scream. "Get off him! Get off him!"

I'm pulling at Cody, who clenches his wiry legs tighter around Glenn's body. With every hit that lands on Glenn's face, Cody bellows.

"Don't…You…Ever…Speak…To…Her…Like…That …Again!"

"Cody! Stop!" I yank at his hood hard, probably choking him. "Please, stop!"

"You *piece*…of *shit*!" Cody yells, spitting into Glenn's bloody face before standing up and walking away. Over his shoulder he yells, "Get him outta here…*Jules*!"

Glenn rolls into fetal position on his side and sobs.

I leave him crying on the driveway and hustle inside, where my charged phone is sitting on my bedside table. I call a local cab company, then head back outside to find Glenn sitting up in the middle of the snowy, gravel driveway, knees bent, face bleeding.

"He's a fucking…*animal*, Juliet," he moans.

I put my hands on my hips. "You provoked him."

"I'll have him arrested," he says.

"The fuck you will, Glenn. He's a decorated Marine. You were trespassing on private property with an intent to stir up trouble. And I'm happy to give that exact account to the sheriff."

"Bitch," he growls softly, tilting his head back. "I think he broke my nose."

I shrug. "You shouldn't have come here."

"Did you not hear me?" he screams. "My nose...is *broken*!"

"I heard you." I force myself not to smile at his pity party for one. "If you want, the cab can take you to the hospital before the airport. They can set your nose."

I sit on the porch behind him, listening to him whine and complain, and thank God when the cab finally pulls up.

"Do you need help getting up?" I ask.

"Get the fuck away from me," he growls, shifting to all fours before standing up. "I better not see you again. Stay away from me when you get back to in Minneapolis."

"With pleasure," I tell him. I can't help adding in a singsong voice: "Get home safely, now."

"Fuck you, Jules," he says, pulling the door shut, but opening the window to add: "Fuck you very much."

***

Cody

Holy shit.

I can't remember a time I was ever as pissed off as I was when that *asshole* said "Fuck you" to my girl. I saw red. I saw white. Then I didn't see anything. I barreled into that fucker and kept hitting until my parka zipper started chafing my neck and I realized that Juliet was physically trying to pull me off of him.

I have no idea what damage I was able to inflict, but I hope it was enough for him to remember his manners the next time he's around a lady.

"Motherfucker!" I yell at the top of my lungs.

I've taken a short hike into the woods behind my house to cool off, but now it's time to go back. I'm sure Juliet is angry with me for losing my cool, and God only knows if that pretentious fucking asshole is gearing up to go into town and press charges for assault. Great. Fantastic. Know what? I don't fucking care. I'll pay a fine. I'll even spend a few nights in jail. It was worth it to teach that arrogant fuck a lesson he had coming.

Oh, and another thing?

I'm going home with Juliet for Christmas.

I saw her face when I said no, and it looked crushed. Well, leave it to guys like Steinbuck to disappoint a girl like her. I'm better than that. I can *do* better than that, *be* better than that. I love her, and when you love someone, you don't say no if there's the slimmest chance you can say yes. Even if it's inconvenient. Even if it doesn't always make sense. Love isn't just in what you say…it's also in what you do.

She wants me to go home with her for Christmas? Fine. I'll go home with her. For four days, the dogs can exercise on their own in the pasture instead of racing. We'll race them harder than ever when we come home.

Yeah, it'll be a big favor to ask from Jonas and Rita, but maybe they'll consider staying out here at my place for a few days. Or maybe I can get Mitch to do it if I pay him a little something. Don't college kids always need extra cash? Whatever it takes, I'll make it work. I'll be sitting next to her on a plane to Missoula come December twenty-third and that's that.

I hike out of the woods just as the sun is setting and take Denver and Concord out of the paddock, locking them back in the kennel. It's almost dinnertime for them, but I want to talk to Juliet first.

I trudge into the house to find her sitting on the couch, parka and boots off, a cup of tea warming her hands, a troubled expression on her beautiful face.

"Hi," I say.

"Hey," she says.

There's an awkward silence between us as I shrug out of my coat and toe off my boots. Finally, she breaks it.

"Glenn left." She pauses, then asks me in a small voice, "Are you...okay?"

"I'm fine," I say, crossing the room to sit down on the coffee table across from her. "Are you?"

She places her tea on the table next to my hip and takes my hands in hers.

"I'm so *sorry*. He's such an asshole. I didn't invite him here."

"I gathered as much," I say, taking a deep breath, then letting it go. "So he was the professor you—"

"Please don't," she says, but then she adds in a whisper, "Yes."

I gulp, because it physically hurts to think about her being with a douchebag like him. No matter who she ends up with—me or someone else—he should treat her like a queen. All the time. Every moment. Even when he's mad. Even when he's furious. He should still treat her with dignity and respect and love.

"I'm glad you're not with him anymore," I say.

"I was barely with him at all," she says. "And we weren't…exclusive. I thought we were, but…"

"That's right. He cheated on you." I blink at her, my brain swirling with murderous thoughts. "Think his plane's left yet?"

"Whoa, boy." Her lips twitch. "You already got him good. He was headed to the hospital when he left…to get his nose set."

Now this is some good news!

"Broken?"

She shrugs, her smile in full bloom now. "Looked that way."

"Yes!" I say, leaning forward to plant my lips on hers. I kiss her gently, tenderly, wanting her to know that I love her, in spite of what happened, that I'd defend her honor a hundred more times if it was required of me. That I will never let her feel unprotected or unloved as long as we're together. Which reminds me…

I draw back just enough to see her eyes, which are dark with arousal.

"Hey darlin'," I say. "I have something to ask you?"

Her voice is dreamy and drunk. "Hmm? What?"

"Is that invitation to go home with you at Christmas still open?"

She gasps, leaning away from me so she can see my whole face. "Y-Yes!"

"Then I'd like to take you up on it."

"Cody! Oh, my God! Cody!" she cries, leaning forward

to throw her arms around my neck. "You mean it? What about the dogs? What about—"

"I'll take care of it," I tell her, wanting her closer to me, but she's still perched on the edge of the couch, and I'm still sitting on the table across from her. I stand up, and she follows my lead. When her body's flush against mine, and my blood's pumping fast and furious to one place, I ask her, "Think we could be a few minutes late giving the dogs dinner tonight?"

"I even think they'd understand," she says, grinning at me as she takes my hand and pulls me back to the bedroom, "just this once."

CHAPTER TWELVE

Juliet

As we touch down in Missoula just before midnight, after a three-leg flight (Nome-Anchorage-Seattle-Missoula), and ten straight hours of travel, I'm exhausted. I had forgotten, after almost three months, how long it takes to get from Nome to…anywhere.

We checked one large suitcase to cut down on extra fees, and after we collect it, we head outside to the curb to find my father, who spots us immediately, beeping the horn on his black GMC Yukon.

"Little Puppy!" he yells from the open passenger window, pulling up alongside of us and jumping out of the car.

"*Little Puppy*?" asks Cody, with raised eyebrows and a curious smile.

I wink at him. "Nickname. I'm Little Puppy. Braydon's Big Puppy."

"O-kaaaay," he says, pulling the suitcase behind him as I run over to my dad.

He pulls me into a bear hug, then leans back to kiss my forehead before hugging me again. My dad smells like dog and cat, antiseptic wash and peppermint. It's a mix of smells among my favorites in the whole world.

"Dad!" I cry, hugging him back.

"You're here. You're home."

"I'm home," I say, leaning back to grin at him.

"Let me look at you!" He cradles my cheeks in his warm, bare hands. "Oh, you look great, honey. Just great."

"You too, Dad." I glance over my shoulder at Cody, who's standing on the curb, watching us. "Dad, you have to meet Cody." I pull away from my father, standing between two of the most important men in my life. "Dad, this is Cody Garrison. Cody, this is my father, Wilbur Sanderson."

"Folks call me Will," says my dad, offering his hand to Cody.

I've warned my parents about Cody's disability, that his right hand, his shaking hand, is severely disfigured and missing fingers. But my father doesn't look down as Cody raises his bare hand to clasp my dad's. He looks straight into Cody's eyes, his warm smile broadening the moment their palms are flush.

"It's good to meet you, sir," says Cody without pulling away.

My father beams, finally letting go of Cody after the length of a normal handshake and not a moment sooner. He puts his hands on his hips, sizing up my boyfriend. "Pup has told me great things about you, Cody."

"You're her hero, sir, so that's quite a compliment."

"You served in the military, huh?"

"Yes, sir. From 2003 to 2006."

"Afghanistan?"

"Yes, sir. I was stationed in Kandahar."

"I'm sorry about what happened to your hands," says my dad. He's direct, but his voice is kind. He acknowledges Cody's disability without speaking down to it.

"I try not to let them slow me down, sir," Cody answers, and while this exchange makes me a little nervous—Cody's hands are a sensitive topic—I'm also impressed by the way my dad and Cody seem to navigate the subject so gracefully.

"Quite literally!" chirps my father. "You race sled dogs!"

"Yes, sir. I do."

"Think Juliet has any promise?"

"Quite a lot, sir," he says, sliding his eyes to mine and offering me a small smile. "I'd go so far as to say she's a natural."

My father claps Cody on the back, then takes the suitcase from beside him, wheeling it to the trunk and encouraging us to get out of the cold and into the car. I take the front seat and Cody gets in the back for the half-hour ride. My parents live in a sprawling six-bedroom home with ten acres of land, a horse barn, paddock and decks with panoramic views of Lolo Peak and the Bitterroot River, about ten miles south of downtown Missoula.

"Can't believe you kids are only here for three nights," my dad grouses.

"That's a lot, Dad. The Qimmiq is in three and a half weeks."

"I know," he says. "Just miss having you around, pup."

"You'll be sick of me by spring," I say, referring to the

ten weeks of internship I'll be doing at my father's veterinary clinic from early April to mid-June.

"No way, no how," he answers. "Cody, who's looking after your dogs this week?"

"My friends, Jonas and Rita, have a college-age son, Mitchell. He's staying at my place."

"Oh, that's great."

"Yeah. He's not a racer, but he'll make sure they're fed and cared for. I have a fenced paddock where he can let them run for exercise."

"Sounds good. I bet they enjoy the break from training too."

"I don't know about that, sir. Sled dogs love racing more than anything else." He pauses. "But when Juliet asked to me come, I didn't want to say no."

My dad raises his eyebrows at me and grins, which makes me blush. I can tell he approves of Cody, and I like that, but it makes me feel bashful too.

"Are, um...are Braydon and Kristy staying over tomorrow night?" I ask.

"Already at the house," my dad says. "But probably asleep."

My brother and his girlfriend share an apartment in downtown Missoula but stay at my parents' house during the holidays. Kristy's folks are from Virginia, but she's not close to them, so my parents have pretty much adopted her.

"You have family missing you this week, Cody?" my dad asks, looking at Cody in the rearview mirror.

"No, sir," he answers. "Not much family to speak of.

My sister lives in California, but we're not close."

"That's too bad."

"She and I are half-siblings," he explains. "She's much older than I am."

"Well, Debbie and I are delighted you decided to join us."

"Thank you, sir. It's been a long time since I had a family Christmas."

"Then brace yourself," my dad says with a chuckle. "Debbie's not known for half-measures."

I look back at Cody, and we share a smile before I turn to my father.

"What's on the docket for tomorrow?" I ask.

"Did I tell you I bought a camp up by Lincoln?"

"What? No!"

"Race to the Sky starts in Lincoln, sir, doesn't it?" asks Cody.

"Sure does, Cody. You ever raced it?"

"No, sir. But I'd like to. Someday."

"Dad," I interrupt. "Tell me about your new place!"

"Oh, yeah. I thought we might go up and see it. It's a little run-down, but in a great location. Two-bedroom cabin. Has plumbing and electricity. Paddock and barn. Both need a little work, but I don't mind that. We're up there every year for the race, not to mention, it's close to Smith Lake. Great—"

"Pike and perch fishing?"

"That's my pup!" says my dad. "You fish, Cody?"

"Not much, sir."

"Willing to give it a try?"

"Yes, sir."

"Cody?" says my dad, flicking a glance in the rearview mirror.

"Yes, sir?"

"I sure do appreciate your manners, son, but if you can see to dropping the 'sir,' I'd really like for us to be friends. What do you say?"

I grin at my dad, before looking over my shoulder at Cody, who nods.

"I'd like that too, sir—um, Will."

***

My dad wasn't kidding about my mom going all-out at Christmas.

The entire house is covered in twinkle lights and decorations: two small Christmas trees roped in white lights on the front porch, and another two just inside the front door. There are five fireplaces in my parent's house and every one of them is dressed with pine boughs, gold bows, and white lights. In the great room, which is two stories high and boasts a massive fieldstone fireplace, there's a decorated Christmas tree almost ten feet tall, and underneath are about a hundred gifts, wrapped in silver and gold, metallic reds and greens. It's like the North Pole in Debbie Sanderson's house, and she's proud of it.

She greets us at the front door with big hugs, then ushers Cody to a guest room and me to my childhood bedroom across the hall. We are informed that just like Braydon and Kristy, who aren't engaged yet, we will be sleeping in separate bedrooms until such time as promises are made.

As I roll my eyes at my mother, I notice Cody's cheeks pinken. Is he thinking of all the things he's done to Will and Debbie's daughter in his bed up in Nome? I sure am. After my parents leave us and head to their main floor master bedroom, I quickly change into my pajamas and knock softly on Cody's door.

He opens it, standing in the doorway to block me from entering.

"Yes?" he asks, trying not to smile.

"Let me in!" I whisper.

"Nope."

"Cody," I say, pushing on his rock-hard abs, "Come on!"

"No, ma'am, I can't. I like your dad too much."

"He likes you too!"

"He won't if he finds his daughter in my bed."

"We can be quiet."

"No, darlin', you can't," he says, that smile getting the better of him.

He calls me "darlin'," and I'm instantly wet, I swear.

"*Please*," I say, pouting a little. I'm not above begging. I *want* him.

"Absolutely not."

"Fine," I say, crossing my arms over my chest and turning away.

In a split second, his arm snakes around my waist, and he turns me to face him. His eyes are dark with longing as his lips land on mine. My arms wind around his neck as he kisses the breath from my lungs, holding me tightly in the upstairs hallway of my parents' house. He laps at my tongue, tangling his with mine as his growing erection grinds against my belly. I whimper softly, and he breaks off the kiss, skimming his lips along my throat.

"Told you."

"Told me what?"

"That you couldn't be quiet."

I chuckle against his shoulder, still holding him, feeling a completeness, a wholeness, a happiness that I've never known with another man. It bubbles up inside of me, fully formed and ready to be spoken, and I'm helpless to repress it, not that I would if I could. It's too full of joy. Too alive. Too much wonderful to keep hidden inside.

"I love you, Cody," I whisper near his ear. "I'm so glad you're here with me."

His arms go slack for a second before tightening around me, then he leans his head up, finding my eyes in the dim light and holding them.

"I love you, too. And there's nowhere else in the world I want to be."

And then he kisses me again, slowly and tenderly this time, so gently that I feel like I'll die if he doesn't let me into his bed or follow me into mine. I take his hand.

"Come with me."

He doesn't move much, just wiggles from my hold, cups my face with his warm hands for the first time ever, and says…

"No."

Then he kisses my forehead, turns around, and closes his door.

And me? I'm left standing in the hallway, frustrated beyond belief, my heart more full than it's ever been, with no other option than to head back to my own bed…alone.

***

We watch *A River Runs through It* after mass and dinner on Christmas Eve, and when it snows on Christmas morning, my brother and I take out the toboggans with Kristy and Cody and go sledding before opening presents.

Cody gives my parents a framed picture of me racing my all-girl team. I have no idea when he took it or how he got it so beautifully framed, but I can tell they're very touched, and my father promises to find it a great place in the waiting room of his office.

To me, he gives a sterling silver husky charm on a sterling silver bracelet, which he clasps lovingly around my wrist, and I promise never to take off. And for the first time I can ever remember, I wonder what it would feel like to receive a smaller jewelry box, holding a ring instead of a bracelet, and something inside of me thrills at the possibility.

Later that evening, after we've packed for our seven o'clock flight and I'm standing on the back deck, looking out over the moonlit mountains, Cody joins me.

"Hey," I say, grinning at him. "Did you finally escape from my father's lecture about giving sled dogs probiotics?"

He smiles, putting his arms around me from behind and resting his chin on my shoulder. "Your dad's an amazing man."

"I agree," I say, covering his gloved hands with mine.

"You were really lucky, Juliet," he says, "to grow up in a family like this one. Your parents are phenomenal. Your brother's awesome. You have it all."

"Now that I have you, I do," I say, leaning back against him.

"Except our lives are going to diverge, come January," he says.

I take a deep breath. "Do they have to?"

"Yeah." His breath is soft and warm against my neck when he speaks. "You go to school in Minneapolis. My home is in Nome. Nineteen dogs, remember?"

"I remember," I say, because I know that his life wouldn't be easy to uproot. Not emotionally, and not actually.

"I can live on what I get from Uncle Sam and the pipeline," he says, referring to his disability pension, which is significant, and the annual payout by the state of Alaska, "but it's not a fancy lifestyle. This house?" he says, "Your parents' lifestyle? I can't offer you that. If that's what you want—"

"I don't know what I want," I say. "I thought I did. I thought I wanted to be a vet in Missoula, working at a family practice with my dad and brother, but now…"

"I think that *is* what you want," I tell her. "I've seen you with your dad…with your brother. You *belong* here. This is your home, darlin'."

I turn around in his arms, unable to keep useless tears

from filling my eyes. It felt so good, so right, to tell Cody I loved him. But what's the use of loving someone if you can't be with them? If you can't build a life with them?

"I don't know how to say good-bye to you," I tell him.

He takes a deep, jagged breath, though his arms stay firm and strong around me. "We don't have to say good-bye yet. Still three weeks and change before the Qimmiq and a few days together after that. We still have four weeks."

"I know, but then…"

"How about we figure out *then* when *then* comes along?" he suggests.

"I'm a planner," I say. "I don't know if I can do that."

"I'm asking you to live in the moment with me," he says, looking deeply into my eyes. "I'm asking you for the next four weeks. Can you give them to me? Because I'll give every second of them to you."

I clench my teeth together and force myself to swallow over the terrible lump in my throat. Can I give them to him? Can I love him totally and absolutely for four weeks, and then walk away from him when it's over?

"I'd rather have four weeks of wonderful than forty years of nothing special," he says. "I'll live on it for the rest of my life."

This man—this good, sweet, strong, kind man who served his country and lost so much—is asking me for time. He's asking me for the gift of time. And I can't—not even to stall the inevitability of my broken heart—say no to him.

"Me too," I whisper, resting my cheek on his shoulder, and imagining our hearts beating in time. "The next four weeks are yours, Cody. All yours."

And may God help me move on with my life when they're over.

***

Cody

She's keeping up with me like a seasoned racer, I think, looking back at Juliet, and her seven-dog team, over my shoulder. It's New Year's Eve, we're back in Nome, and I think we're *almost* ready for the Qimmiq.

She's got the commands down pat: "Gee" for "go right," "Haw" for "go left," "Whoa" for "stop," and "Easy" for "slow down." My girls already knew the commands, but listening for them from *Juliet*, and following *her* instructions, took them a couple of weeks to gel. They accept her as their musher now. And damn, but it's exciting to see.

As we race through the miles and miles of snow-covered trails behind my house, building up our endurance and bonding with our teams, I have plenty of time to think.

And despite my pleas to live in the moment, all I think about is the future.

Like most teenaged boys, the idea of getting married and having kids was a terrifying prospect to be avoided by double-bagging my wang and triple checking that my partner was on birth control. No way I wanted to be pinned down by premature fatherhood.

And by the time normal thoughts of a wife and children would have emerged—in my late twenties or early thirties—I had completely dispelled the notion of finding someone who would accept me as I am.

But underneath it all—in the deepest and most desperately lonely recesses of my heart—I always wanted what I didn't have: to be part of a nuclear family, with a stable mother and father, and happy kids to whom my wife and I provide a loving, nurturing childhood.

Since meeting Juliet, I find that long-suppressed desire softly and tentatively reasserting itself. She loves me and I love her, and the idea of creating a life with her—*a child*—is so heady that sometimes the very fantasy can steal my breath away.

"Haw! Haw!" she yells, and I look up to see Cheyenne turn right, her neon-green booties moving so fast against the white snow, they're a blur. Olympia and Phoenix, strong dogs and militant rule followers, pull the rest of the team in the direction Cheyenne chooses, and Helena, ably anchoring the sled, keeps the raw strength of Augusta and Juneau from leading the whole team astray on a whim. It's a tight configuration, and my girl handles it effortlessly.

What would this look like as a…life? I indulge the fantasy for a moment, letting my brain conjure sweet images of a life with Juliet: racing together all over Alaska and the northern United States, two little ones whom we teach how to handle the dogs. She could maybe get a job working with Jonas—Lord knows he has his hands full now and then and would probably welcome another vet stepping in to help. We could make the loft into a nursery for the kids and spend nights in front of the fire making love. Summer days on the beach, sticking our feet in the Bering Sea, and yearly visits to her family in Montana.

My fantasies come skidding to a halt right there.

I remember Juliet's joyful reunion with her father at the airport and the way her mother greeted us at the front door of their house. Braydon and Juliet have a tight bond, I recall, remembering them racing toboggans down a snowy hill. Once a year with her family wouldn't be enough—wouldn't be *nearly* enough, either for her or, I realize with some surprise, for me.

Her family is a concrete foundation. It was the beginning that gave Juliet the character, strength, and confidence to be the woman she is. Her father's good humor, kindness, and love. Her mother's ethics, nurturing, and cheerfulness. Would I want to raise my own family with such limited access to the one that created a person as marvelous as Juliet? Once a year just wouldn't be enough.

But the flights from Nome to Missoula aren't cheap, I have a responsibility to my dogs, and I don't have unlimited resources. I paid for my house outright, and I don't carry any debt. But I get just under forty thousand dollars a year in disability pay from the federal government and another two thousand dollars a year from the state of Alaska. Living frugally on that amount means I don't have to get a job, not that I'd be well-qualified for much anyway, since I have such limited use of my hands in most conventional settings.

That said, a guy from the Nome Visitor's Center corners me at the Klondike at least once or twice a year and asks me if I'd be interested in offering Sled Dogs Visits and Tours. He claims he can charge $299 for a three-hour tour,

80 percent of which is mine to keep and promises that he could book a minimum of a three dozen tours per year. I turn him down every time, because I'm really not interested in a bunch of strangers turning up at my place year-round to gawk at my hands and mess up my training schedule. But now I wonder if an additional ten thousand dollars a year might be worth a little inconvenience. Hmm.

"Whoa! Whoa, girls!"

Ahead of me Juliet stops her team to take a drink from her water bottle. The girls lounge or roll in the snow, ready to keep going but also getting weary after a four-and-a-half-hour workout.

"Whoa, boys!" I stop my team beside hers. "You're looking good, woman."

She's red cheeked and out of breath. "Oh, yeah?"

I nod. "Oh, yeah. Love watching you go."

"I love racing," she says. "But I'm nervous about three straight days and two nights on the trail. It's a lot."

"Yeah. But I'll be carrying most of the overnight supplies, and I'll stick close to you. Remember, we don't have to win. We just have to finish. We can take our time."

"I know. But the nights...the distance...I'm just...I hope I'm ready."

"Next week," I tell her, throwing meat strips to the dogs, "we'll do a couple more overnights, okay? You'll be fine by January thirteenth. I promise, darlin'."

She grins at me, chewing on a piece of reindeer jerky. "Hey, you know how it's New Year's Eve?"

"Uh-huh."

"Well, I was thinking we could feed the dogs as soon as we get in—you know, get it over with—and then maybe, instead of going to the Klondike, we could stay in? Have some dinner…drink some wine…maybe watch a movie?"

"You don't want to go out? Are you tired?"

She shrugs, looking down, but before she does, I catch the furrow in her brow, the frown lines around her lips. "Race is in thirteen days. I leave in twenty-one. I think I just want you to myself as much as possible between then and now."

"Then let's stay in," I tell her. "Just you and me."

***

I make steaks and baked potatoes for dinner, followed by ice cream with chocolate sauce, and Juliet chooses *Shakespeare in Love* for our after-dinner viewing pleasure, saying that she needs to watch the movie that inspired my favorite dog's name.

But spooned on the couch, with the beautiful love story playing out on the screen in front of us, I can *feel* her melancholy. When we were in Montana last week, standing outside on the deck, I asked her to live in the now with me. But I'm realizing, day by day, that that was a selfish and unfair request. She is a self-proclaimed planner, and by asking her to "live in the moment," I was also asking her to shut up about the future. Asking someone not to talk about something doesn't mean it isn't eating away at them every moment. I can *feel* her sadness and despair, and my request is forcing her to bear it alone, rather than sharing it with me.

I turn off the TV when the credits start rolling. We're

alone in the dark room, the potbelly stove casting shadows on the wall.

"Flip over," I say. "I want to talk to you."

When she does, her face is a mask of sorrow, and I am furious with myself for letting things get to this point.

"About what?" she asks, her voice thin and weary.

"The future."

She blinks at me. "You asked me not to. You want to live in the now."

I shake my head. "Not anymore. Talk to me, Juliet."

"I t-tried," she says softly, "not to think about January twenty-second, when I'm back at school, and you're here all alone getting ready for the Iditarod, but—I'm so sorry, Cody—I can't stop thinking about it. We have no plan to ever see each other again after I leave…but I love you. I c-can't…bear it."

I lean forward and press my lips to hers. "I'm so sorry I made you keep this all inside."

"I'm not asking for—for, you know, a ring or a—oh, God!—anything like that. I just…just want to know we'll *see* each other again."

"Of course we will," I tell her.

"How?" she asks. "How does that look? I'm in Minneapolis until early April, then I'm working at my dad's practice until June. Then back to Minneapolis for graduation."

"Okay," I say. "Maybe we plan to get together in June? After your graduation?"

"Five months?" she asks, her eyes wide and glassy.

"That's a *long* time!"

Agreed. "Hmm. Do you have a spring break?"

"Um…yeah. In March. I think it's the ninth to the thirteenth."

I take a deep breath, and my eyes shutter closed.

"What?" she asks. "What is it?"

"That's the Iditarod. It starts on the seventh."

Her face falls. "So you'll be busy the week I'm free."

"You could volunteer," I suggest.

She clenches her jaw together, on the verge of tears, because she knows as well as I do that I won't have a moment to spare with her whether she volunteers or not.

"I—I could ask Jonas and Rita to watch the dogs again in April," I say quickly. "When you go back to Montana, I could come and spend a few days."

"Sure…" she says, her voice resigned. "We can spend a few days together every few months."

"Once you graduate," I say, "you could come back. You could spend the whole summer here."

She stares at me intently for a moment, and for a second, I can almost see her mind whirring. "Or you could come to Montana and spend the summer with me."

"But the dogs—"

"Bring them," she says quickly, looking me dead in the eyes, a slight challenge in her expression. "Fly them to Anchorage and drive them down to Missoula. I'll come back and help you." She lips her lips. "Oh, my God, Cody! I didn't even think of it…but we could stay at my dad's cabin in Lincoln! The horse paddock could be used for the dogs…we could even help him spruce it up a little while we're—"

"Juliet, I don't even know if it's drivable from—"

"It is! I've checked," she says. "You can drive from Anchorage to Montana. Through Canada. No problem."

"It's got to be three thousand miles."

"Twenty-five hundred," she says. "Six days. Four hundred and twenty miles a day…give or take."

"You've been looking into this," I say.

"I won't lie to you," she tells me. "I've been looking into *anything* that would buy us more time together, though I hadn't thought about the cabin until now. I'd been thinking in terms of us staying at my parents' house…which is its own kind of torture."

I'm still trying to get my head around her plan. "You want me to bring my dogs to Missoula this spring?"

She nods. "Yes."

"And then what?"

"I'll help you bring them back here in the fall."

I lean up on my elbow. "Let me just get this straight…You're suggesting I fly myself and my dogs to Anchorage, buy a mobile kennel, buy a truck, meet you, drive six days through the Canadian wilderness, and live a few months at your father's cabin in Montana before doing the whole thing again."

She gulps softly. "Yes."

I can't help it.

I laugh.

I laugh at her because this idea is so ridiculous, so

impossible.

"Juliet! Do you have any idea what that would cost?"

"Well, I—"

"Flights for me and the dogs to Anchorage? Over three thousand dollars, easy."

"That sounds extreme."

"It's not. It's part of what I have saved up to get to the starting line at the Iditarod," I tell her. "A truck? Even used, but decent enough to make that journey? A good ten thousand dollars. A Dog Box with twenty kennels and a hitch for transport? Another fifteen hundred dollars. Not to mention the trip itself—hotels and meals for us and them? More money I *do not have*!" I stare at her for a second. "Are you kidding or crazy?"

"Crazy, I guess." Her face goes blank, and she wiggles out of my arms, sitting up and putting her back to me. She continues softly: "Unless we win the Qimmiq. The purse is ten thousand dollars."

"We can't—" I rub my face with my hands. "Juliet. We cannot win the Qimmiq. We're rookies."

"Right," she murmurs, standing up. "Dumb idea. Crazy me."

I hear her footsteps recede down the back hall and instantly feel like a monumental asshole for crushing her dreams. But seriously? Seriously? Her plan is crazy. It's totally nuts, right?

I have ten thousand dollars saved up to enter the Iditarod. That'll cover the cost of getting me, my sled, and my dogs to Anchorage the night before the race, and everything I need—both on my sled and for checkpoint drop bags—to race back to Nome. It's all I've got saved for this. The rest of my money is allocated toward my everyday expenses: food for me and my dogs, maintenance on my home, my truck, gas, et cetera. I definitely do not have an extra fifteen thousand dollars lying around to spend on a Montana vacation, no matter how much I want to be with Juliet. It's ludicrous. Impossible.

Except it's not, whispers my heart. *If you win the Qimmiq and open a line of credit for the truck, you could swing it.*

But winning the Qimmiq?

No way.

There are seasoned racers signed up, mushers who've been racing for years. Juliet's been racing for a handful of months. And me? I shake my head. *It's just not possible. It's not.*

No matter how much we want it, there are better racers.

I stand up and trek back to the bedroom, where I find her curled up on the bed with her back to the door.

"Hey," I say. "I'm sorry I called you crazy."

She doesn't face me so her voice is muffled when she speaks: "You've lived with 'good-enough' for so long, you barely dare to dream of spectacular."

"What does that mean?"

"You don't have any hope!" she cries, flipping over to face me with a tear-streaked face. "Would it be hard to win the Qimmiq? Would we be long shots? Yes and yes. But impossible? No way, Cody. We just have to come up with the right strategy."

"You've never raced before!"

"I know that!"

I stare at her, feeling like my head's about to explode.

"Nor have I ever fallen in love before…or raced sled dogs before…or wanted anything in my whole life as much as I want you," she says. "But somehow those things are all happening. Just because something wonderful hasn't happened yet, doesn't mean it can't!"

"You want to win the Qimmiq," I say, staring into her bright blue eyes.

"I want to *try*," she says, sniffling softly.

I run what's left of my fingers through my hair. "It's two-hundred miles."

"I know."

"You're only comfortable doing fifty a day."

"I can do more," she says, sitting up.

"Seventy? Eighty?"

She nails me with those blue eyes. "Are you willing to consider coming to Montana this summer?"

I bite my bottom lip, then lick it. I feel nervous, but I can't deny it: there's this galvanizing momentum, this insane-*fucking*-energy budding within me. I can feel it taking root. I can feel it dying to grow.

"This is crazy," I tell her.

She wipes away her tears, nodding at me with a blossoming smile. "Yes. It's crazy. Be crazy with me."

"I don't know if we can win," I tell her, searching her eyes.

"We'll never know if we don't try," she tells me,

breathing deeply.

I take a deep breath too, holding it for a second before letting it go. "Okay. Okay, we'll... we'll train harder. We'll...see what we can do. We'll try!"

"Cody!" she cries, rising up on her knees and opening her arms.

I embrace her, letting her pull me onto the bed with her. I kiss her face all over, the maniacal notion that two rookie mushers could actually *win* a race, a plan I've got to try. For her. For my Juliet. Only for my love.

Grinning at me, she reaches for her phone, flipping it over to show me the time: 12:03 a.m.

"Happy New Year, Cody," she says.

"Here's to the future, darlin'," I tell her, fusing my lips to hers, and praying that our hope and our conviction is enough to make a miracle happen.

CHAPTER THIRTEEN

Juliet

"Wake up," Cody whispers. "Juliet. Wake up. We gotta get going. Come on. Get up."

It's Day #2 of the Qimmiq and pitch-dark in our icy-cold tent.

My body aches everywhere.

My face and fingers feel both dry *and* frozen.

My eyes will barely open, and when I force them, they burn.

Why is he waking me up already? I couldn't have slept for more than ten minutes.

"What time is it?" I mutter.

"Four."

"Already?"

"Yep. You got three hours of sleep, but we've got to go now if we want to get a jump on the lead."

"Cody," I half whisper, half sob, as I try to sit up, "I'm *so* tired."

"I know," he says, putting his arm around my waist to steady me when it looks like I might topple over. "But we did the mandatory six-hour rest. If we want to win…"

"O-Okay," I say, rubbing my eyes. "Okay. I'm up. I'm up."

"Eat." He hands me a piece of reindeer jerky and a Ziploc bag of dried fruit. "They've got some great volunteers here. Got the dogs fed in half an hour."

I can hear them, not too far away from where I got a little sleep in our tent, baying and howling.

"A guy helped with the harnesses too. Checked yours and mine. They're ready to run again."

Once the volunteers at the Qimmiq found out about Cody's military service and disability, they immediately started championing us. When we arrived at the Teller checkpoint five hours ago, the cheering was deafening, and we seemed to be prioritized over other arriving teams by the waiting volunteers.

"Vet checked on Boston's paw. Wrapped it up and got the bootie back on. Looks okay to go again today."

"How many miles left?" I ask.

"Uh…little over a hundred," he says.

"How many *exactly*?"

"A hundred and twenty-two."

The Qimmiq 200 started yesterday in Nome and continued northeast to Teller. Today, we'll follow the shoreline of the Imuruk Basin to the abandoned village of Mary's Igloo, and continue southeast to Council. On Monday, we'll end up back in Nome at the same finish line used by Iditarod racers.

Our strategy was to do eighty miles in ten hours on the first day with one break at the first checkpoint halfway between Nome and Teller, then stop for sleep at the second checkpoint, just southeast of Teller. I don't know how exactly, because I could barely feel my extremities by the time we arrived in Teller, but somehow, we made it.

Today we're supposed to do the same, stopping at Mary's Igloo to eat and let the dogs take a three-hour rest, but *we* won't set up camp and sleep until after the fifth checkpoint, in Council. Then we'll finish the final fifty miles tomorrow, hopefully arriving first in Nome.

Except I can barely sit up. How am I going to mush a team for another rigorous day and a half?

Cody hands me another piece of jerky. "I got some cheesecake too. You want it?"

I nod. "Uh-huh."

It's a weird combination of foods we're using to keep our strength and stamina up: protein, of course, like jerky, which wears well on the trail, and dried fruit, which shatters like glass when I bite down because it's so cold, but cheesecake is also great. Even if it freezes, it tastes delicious as it thaws in my mouth and has tons of fat and sugar for a quick energy burst.

"Who else is here right now?" I ask.

"Everyone except one team. Heard them leave about thirty minutes ago. I checked and our times from yesterday have us at fourth right now. We need to make up some time today and tomorrow."

I blink at him, trying not to cry. "We need to *make up* time?"

Cody's eyes are sympathetic. "If we want to win. Yes."

It's the reminder—the push—I need, and I nod, shoving a chunk of cheesecake in my mouth and crawling out of the tent, onto the hay-covered snow.

It's got to be thirty below out here.

And it's dark as midnight.

But the air is bracingly brackish from the wind sweeping in from the Bering Sea. I take a deep breath and the cold burns my lungs, but not in a bad way; in a way that wakes me up after the rigors of yesterday's mushing and so little sleep last night.

I knew that sleep deprivation would be part of these three days of racing, and when Cody and I agreed to make a run for first place, I knew it could be even more brutal than I'd originally planned. That said, our financial resources are decidedly limited, and the Qimmiq purse is imperative to our future.

My parents were generous enough to pay for grad school and give me a small allowance, but I can't ask them for more money to help relocate my Alaskan boyfriend to Montana for a few months. And from what Cody tells me, his extra savings have all been ear-marked for the Iditarod.

Winning the Qimmiq would mean everything to our relationship.

Without it, he could maybe come and visit me for a few days in June, and I could maybe fly up to Nome a few months later for a visit with him after I'd been working for a while and earned up a few vacation days. But it wouldn't be a good plan for maintaining the intimacy of our relationship. I'm just not sure how Cody and I—as a relatively new couple—would survive.

I stand up, my boots crunching over the snow and ice

as Cody leads the way to our harnessed teams.

Bending down, I say good morning to each dog individually, giving her a kiss on the muzzle and telling her what a great job she's doing. Something important I've learned during the last three months is that these dogs clock my mood at every turn. If I'm upset, they're nervous. If I'm angry, they're manic. If I'm cheerful and encouraging, they'll run their hearts out for me. We are symbiotic in that way; we need each other to race…and to win.

Stepping onto the back of my sled, I take the reins in hand, then nodding once to Cody to let him know I'm ready, I yell, "Mush!" into the early morning darkness.

***

Arriving at Mary's Igloo this morning before all but one team gave us a good advantage, as did checking in at Council by five o'clock tonight. We blow past the checkpoint, continuing south toward Nome, but by six-thirty, I'm running on fumes and can barely keep my eyes open.

We're in the lead now, but I tell Cody I need to stop.

Because we're between Council and Nome, and not at a checkpoint, there are no volunteers to help us unharness the dogs, bed and feed them, so it takes hours to get them settled.

It's only fifty miles to Nome, a distance we regularly practiced on training days. It's even possible we can make it without stopping, but we need to be sure the dogs get a solid rest before we ask them to run again.

"What are we thinking? Five hours? Six?" I ask Cody.

He's spreading out a layer of hay for our tent. "I

overheard the other team say they were staying at Council until morning. I say we get five hours of sleep, get up, make breakfast for the dogs, and shoot down to Nome."

"Sounds good."

"I'm starving," Cody says. "What do *we* have?"

I take out four vacuum-packed pieces of pizza we picked up in our drop bag at Council, relieved that they haven't frozen between there and here. Cody joins me inside the tent, unrolling and unzipping two sleeping bags so that one can be our mattress and the other our blanket.

"Pizza," I say, handing him two slices.

He gobbles it down hungrily, stopping between bites to ask me: "Can you…set an…alarm?"

I nod, fishing my phone out of the pocket of my parka. "Sure."

Except…my phone isn't there. I put down the pizza and try my other pocket, frantically fishing around for my phone, but it's not there either.

"When did you last use it?" asks Cody.

"On the trail," I say. "To tell you I needed to rest."

"Twenty minutes back," he says.

"Twenty minutes *by sled!*" I say, which translates to two to three miles over land.

"I can go back for it."

"What? How?"

"Snowshoes," he says. "I keep a pair on my sled."

"Cody, that's crazy! That's a four- to six-mile round-trip hike. On no sleep." I stare at him, shaking my head back and forth. "And there's no moon out. No. Forget it. I'm sure someone else will find it and turn it in at the finish line."

"How are we going to communicate tomorrow?" he asks.

Cody had our phones outfitted with SatSleeves before the Qimmiq, so we could get in touch with one another, no matter where we were.

"We can…stay together."

He exhales loudly, with barely concealed annoyance, as he opens his second piece of pizza. "Our whole strategy for tomorrow was for me to push my dogs as hard as possible to bring down our average time."

"Okay…" I say, blinking my eyes at him. I've never been this exhausted in my life. My whole body hurts. My phone is gone. And now Cody's upset with me. "You can still do that. It's only fifty miles. I can do fifty miles solo. Go as fast as you can. I'll see you in Nome."

"No, Juliet," he says with an edge in his voice. "That's not safe. You can't race fifty miles in the wilderness by yourself after two long days and almost no sleep."

"Yes, I can," I tell him, my voice soft and small. "I'll be fine."

"You're not thinking straight. All of the supplies are with me."

"I'll take some on my sled."

"Just…" He finishes his pizza, sets an alarm on his phone, then lies down on his back. "No. We'll stay together. It's safest, but…"

"But what?"

"I don't see how we can win," he says. "You're already

down a dog by having a single lead, which makes you a little slower anyway. If I slow down so we can stay together—"

"Just leave me behind!" I yell.

I lie on my side with my back to him, hating the tears that slide form the corners of my eyes. I don't even remember dropping my phone. I'm so weary and bleary-eyed at this point, so cold and achy. I only had three months to prepare for a race that takes most athletes years of conditioning. All I want to do is crawl into a soft bed and sleep for days, and instead I'm here, somewhere in the middle of Alaska, and the one person anchoring me to this race is mad at me.

Cody rolls onto his side and pulls me against him, and though I'm grateful for the contact, I'm frustrated with him. Can't he see I'm trying my best?

"I didn't mean to drop my phone," I murmur.

"I know."

"I can race alone."

"No darlin'," he says gently, squeezing me tighter, "you can't."

"I'm s-so…s-sorry…Co-dy," I mumble, my eyes fluttering closed as he holds on to me.

"Shhhh," he hums near my ear. "Just sleep."

I do exactly as he says.

***

"Juliet!" Cody's voice is urgent as he shakes me. "Shit! Juliet!"

"Huh? What?"

"The—the other team…they just passed us."

"What? What do you mean?"

"I heard them! Someone yelled, 'Mush!' so I peeked outside and there they were, sliding by."

"What…what time is—"

"Just after midnight," he says. "I mis-judged their rest-time in Council. I think they only took three hours, not six."

I sit up, pushing past the aching pain of every muscle. "We have to…to go. We can catch up. Cody, we can still—"

"No."

His phone light is on, illuminating the tent, and his face says it all: *It's too late. We've already lost.*

"Dogs aren't even harnessed," he says. "But more important, do you hear anything?"

I don't. Nothing but the whistling Arctic wind outside.

"They'd be barking and howling their heads off if they were rearing to go right now. That last leg was five hours long, and we've only been asleep for three. They're tired. They need rest. I need rest. You need rest. I just…" He clenches his eyes shut. "It's over."

"It's okay," I say, my voice lacking any conviction.

"It's not," he answers, turning off the light, his voice laced with misery. "We were so close. We could have—damn it, Juliet, we could have won."

"Lie down with me." When he does, I lean my head forward until my forehead gently touches his in the darkness. "When you asked me to race with you back in September, all you needed was for us to finish. Not win. Not place. Not show. Finish. And we're still going to do that. Maybe not first, but we'll finish."

"But the money…"

"It was long shot anyway," I say. "This was our first race. We were up against seasoned pros." I gulp, concentrating on the one place on my entire body where his skin touches mine. "But we'll still finish, Cody. I promise we'll finish tomorrow…and your dream will come true: you'll race in your first Iditarod this March. And I'll—I'll finish my study and maybe get published. That's why we found each other in the first place, right? That's what's important, right?"

I hear him take a sharp breath, but he doesn't answer.

"And…" I clear my throat, trying to be brave. "We can figure out the rest. We'll plan to see each other in June. Or July. At some point. When we can. Right?"

"Yeah. Right," he says, but his voice is dull and flat. It scares me because it says so much more than his words. He doesn't see our future clearly, and the truth is, neither do I.

"Let's just…s-sleep," I say, turning over so my back is against his chest, and glad he can't see the tears sliding down my cheeks.

"I love you, Juliet," he says softly, his voice gruff with emotion. "Always remember that. No matter what happens. Remember I loved you."

Remember I loved you.

I can't answer because I'm crying too hard and trying not to break into runaway sobs. I swallow my cries and clench my teeth against whimpers. And at some point, my burning eyes close and I finally fall back to sleep in the dark wilderness of Alaska, utterly alone, though my love sleeps beside me.

***

Cody

Fourth place.

We didn't win, place *or* show in the Qimmiq.

We ended up in fourth.

Two more teams passed us on Monday: one in the early morning, before we woke up, and another as we were breaking down camp and harnessing the dogs.

We arrived in Nome at noon.

As the top-placing *local* team, Nome celebrated our fourth-place finish as glorious. Jonas and Rita wouldn't let us pay for celebratory drinks at the Klondike, and the *Nome Nugget* took our picture with the dogs and featured us on its front page the following day: *ROOKIES FROM NOME TAKE 4TH IN THE QIMMIQ!*

But for me and Juliet, time was slipping away like the last bits of sand in an hourglass—and everyone knows the last grains always go the fastest.

Last night, we fed the dogs as soon as we got home and fell into bed by five o'clock. We slept for thirteen hours, waking up at six this morning to feed the dogs breakfast.

We don't speak much as we feed them, perhaps because we're both still a little exhausted from the race, but also because it's difficult to discuss disappointment. It's hard to put heartbreak into words. And though I desperately try not to watch the clock, I hear its nonstop ticking in my head: it's Tuesday morning, and Juliet leaves on Thursday. Our time together is almost at an end.

And sometimes, when it rains, it pours.

Jonas shows up midmorning to return Viola, whom I asked him to watch for the three days we were racing, and I can tell, from one look at his troubled face, that something's wrong.

"Hey, Cody," he says, leaning over the chain-link kennel fence as I finish changing the dogs' hay.

"Hey, Jonas."

"Get some rest last night?"

I nod. "Thirteen hours."

"Whew!" he says. "Bet you feel more yourself this morning."

I scan my friend's face, cutting to the chase. "Jonas, what's going on? You look…"

"Yeah," he says, his smile fading. "I need to talk to you."

"About…?"

"Viola."

Surprised, my eyes slip to her, sitting obediently at his feet.

"Sure," I say, casting a look back at Juliet, who's pushing the food cart back into the grub shack.

When I slip from the kennel enclosure, my eyes slide to Jonas's, and I feel it in my bones: that terrible sense of foreboding when you're about to get very bad news.

"What's going on?"

"About Viola…have you, uh…you noticed her moving slower lately?"

I squat down and take off my gloves with my teeth,

then plunge my hands into Vi's ruff, scratching her neck as best I can with what I've got. The answer to his question is "yes," but I can't bear to say it.

"What's up, Jonas?" I ask in a gravelly voice.

He tightens his jaw for a second. "Let's talk inside."

"No," I say, sitting back on my butt next to Viola. "Here's good. Just tell me."

"There's blood in her stool. I only noticed it because our backyard's so small and snowy." He takes a deep breath. "I tested her, and it's cancer, Cody. Likely started in the spleen, but it's affecting her liver and lungs now, too." He pauses, then adds: "She's got tumors everywhere."

"Jonas!" greets Juliet, joining us at the fence. "Thanks for the drinks yesterday!"

"Hey, Juliet," he says.

I don't look up at her. If I do, I'll cry. Instead, I sit next to Vi, who lies down on the snow and places her head on my thigh. Behind her ears is her softest fur, and my fingers—my stubby, melted fingers that never bothered her a bit—scratch gently.

"Is she...in pain?" I whisper.

"What? Who? What's going on?" asks Juliet from above me. "What...what's happening here?"

Jonas sighs, the sound heavy. "Viola's sick. Stage four spleen cancer."

"Wh-what? No." Juliet's voice holds all the heartbreak I feel. "Wh—How do you know? Are you sure?"

"Yeah. I did an ultrasoun—"

"What about a splenectomy?"

"It's already in her liver and lungs. I found blood in her stool and her urine."

Juliet inhales sharply. "Oh, my God."

There's no gulping over the lump in my throat, no swallowing it down. I stroke Vi's head gently. "How long?"

Jonas clears his throat. "A month. Maybe…less."

Juliet whimpers above me, and I finally slide my eyes to hers, ignoring the wetness of tears on my cheeks.

"Don't cry, darlin'."

"Oh, Cody," she sobs, surging through the gate and dropping to her knees in the snow in front of me. "I'm so, s-so s-sorry, Cody." She reaches out and places her palm gingerly on Vi's back. "Oh, Viola."

"What should I do?" I ask her.

I'm asking the human being I love and trust most in the world if I should put down my dog—my beloved dog, the dog who saved my life and was my constant and loyal companion during the loneliest days I've ever known. I'm asking her to make this decision for me, because I'm not sure I can bear to make it myself.

"Is she in pain?" Juliet reaches up to swipe at tears as she looks at Jonas. "Do you think she's in any pain?"

"Hard to say." Jonas shrugs. "She doesn't whimper or cry in her sleep. She's losing blood for certain, but I've seen worse. Some dogs with her condition will get weaker and more light-headed until they pass away in their sleep. Others—"

"Where is she?" I ask. "In the process of dying?"

"She's still eating small meals. She moves slowly so

there's probably some discomfort, but I can give her something for that. I think it's okay to hold onto her a little longer. Couple more weeks. You'll know when it's time to say good-bye."

Couple more weeks.

Juliet sniffles softly. "Poor Viola."

"Worst part of this job," says Jonas.

I finally look up at my friend. "Couldn't have been easy to tell me."

"I thought to tell you yesterday, but I didn't want to ruin your celebration."

Juliet stands up and places a hand on Jonas's arm. "You're a good friend."

"Don't feel so much like one today." He shrugs sadly. "Carry her up and down steps when you can, Cody. Don't let her jump up or down on furniture or she could further rupture the tumor. Small meals. Sweet words. You can give her a couple of good weeks before you have to say good-bye."

"Okay," I tell him, nodding that I understand his instructions.

"Speaking of good-byes," says Juliet, "I'm going to miss you."

"When do you head home?"

"Thursday," she says, and I never knew before that moment that a day of the week could be a dagger in my heart. "My flight leaves at eight thirty."

"Try to stop by the Klondike and say good-bye to Rita before you go. She'll want to wish you well."

"I'll try," she says, hugging Jonas before stepping away.

I move Viola's head gently from my leg and stand up to shake hands with my friend. "Thanks for looking after her, Jonas."

"I'm so sorry, Cody. Hate like hell that I'm the bearer of sad news."

"Aw," I murmur softly, blinking my eyes like crazy as they well with more tears. "If, uh…if it had to be said, I'm glad it came from um…from you."

I lean back down, slowly picking up my sweet, old friend as tenderly as I can, and holding her against my chest like a baby. My cheeks are probably still glistening with tears. I don't care. I feel like I'm losing everything that matters in my life at once, and it sucks.

Jonas heads back to his car.

I turn around with my dog and walk into my house.

***

Juliet makes a special bed for Viola in my room, on the green carpet, by the stove. It's the two pillows from her bed upstairs covered with the white, furry blanket from the bean bag chair. She gently coaxes Vi to lie down in the little nest, and she does, immediately closing her eyes to sleep.

"You should start using this door to let her go outside," says Juliet, gesturing to the external door in my room. "Maybe we could get a baby gate and block off the back deck, so she doesn't have to use stairs. She can do her business on the deck and we'll just, you know, pick it up for her."

"Yeah. Okay," I say. "I'll go to AC's tomorrow. They'll

have something."

I sit down on the edge of the bed, watching Viola sleep. Juliet sits down next to me, taking one of my hands in hers and putting her head on my shoulder.

"I know how much she means to you," she whispers. "I'm so sorry."

I want her sympathy, but I need her comfort too. The comfort of her body moving against mine, of being buried to the hilt in her warm wetness, of knowing that I am loved when I feel so fucking sad.

"Kiss me," I whisper. "I need you."

Her hands, so soft and warm, land on my cheeks, covering the tears drying there as her eyes look deeply into mine.

"I'm here."

She leans forward, her lips touching mine tenderly as she reaches for the zipper on my coat and pulls it down. As she smooths it over my shoulders, I reach behind my neck with both hands and take off my flannel and T-shirt, throwing them on the ground and deepening our kiss. Her fingers land on the button of my jeans, and she flicks it open, unzipping the fly just as quickly.

Breaking off our kiss, she stands up and undresses quickly as I push my jeans to the floor and draw her naked body into my arms.

"I love you," I say. "I've never loved anyone like this. You're it for me, Juliet. Forever. For the rest of my life, it's only you."

She sobs, pressing her body against mine as I fall back

on the bed, taking her with me. We kiss passionately, her tears salting our lips as she straddles my hips and lowers herself onto me, guiding my erection into her body.

When we are connected as intimately as possible, she sits up straight and looks down at me. "I love you, too. So much, Cody."

I reach for her hips, guiding her back and forth across my hips, impaling her to the hilt, then sliding her back.

"We will find each other again," I promise her. "Hold on."

"I'll…hold on," she says, arching her back, her amazing tits full and flushed, her nipples pert in the morning light that streams through my bedroom window. "I promise."

"We'll figure this out," I tell her, sitting up so that I can look into her eyes while we make love.

Her ankles wrap around my waist and her arms loop around my neck as I continue to thrust upward, into the sweet heaven of her body.

Her lips linger on my neck, pressing against my pulse, resting on my heart.

"Tell me we'll be alright," I beg her, dropping my forehead to her shoulder as I surge into her again.

I can feel the muscles deep inside of her start to convulse around my cock, and she whimpers softly by my ear as she murmurs, "I love you. That's all I know for sure."

My arms are around her as she climaxes, and I am not long behind her, crying out her name as I come in jerking waves of bliss.

"I love you…I love you…I love you too."

Afterward, we lie in bed, holding each other close and desperately hoping that our love is strong enough for the separation that lies ahead.

CHAPTER FOURTEEN

Two Weeks Later

Juliet

I miss him.

It is a constant ache in my heart.

A bitter emptiness within me.

I miss his voice and his face.

I miss the unique clasp of his hand.

I miss his warm body next to mine.

I miss caring for the dogs and sharing our meals together.

I miss the wind in my hair and the whisper of my sled in the snow.

I even miss the Klondike and shopping trips to AC's and Rita's pizza.

But most of all, I just miss Cody. His strong, gentle presence in my life.

We talked on the phone a few times our first week apart, but the conversations were so sad and stilted, and threw me into such a depression after hanging up, I'd lose a whole evening to tears when I should have been studying or writing up my study.

I finally texted him and asked him not to call me for a

little while, and he agreed.

But when I think about him in Nome, with his beloved Viola dying before his very eyes, it makes me want to buy a ticket with money I don't have, screw my fellowship, fuck graduation, and be there to comfort him. I love him. I'm wracked with guilt that I'm not supporting him.

Except I worked for eight years to graduate from veterinary school, and I'm almost finished. I can't quit now. And something tells me he wouldn't let me anyway.

At least for the short-term, I need to get used to being *here* again. I need to figure out a way to live day-by-day without Cody. I need to figure out a way to toughen up about the distance between us. And if I can't...maybe I need to let him go. That's what Sil says, anyway.

"Juliet, this isn't healthy. I know you liked him a lot, but—"

"I didn't just 'like him a lot,'" I try to explain to her. "I love him. Present tense."

"But you don't even know when you'll see him again! I mean, you've got no plan. No future. What are you going to do? Move to *Nome*?"

"This, from a lifetime subscriber of *The Odds Are Good*!" I exclaim. "Need I remind you that this entire plan was *your* idea?"

"I *never* would have chosen a guy in Nome," she tells me, which certainly sounds like a different tune from the one she sang back in September. "Anchorage? Yes. Juneau? Maybe. Ketchikan or Sitka? Sigh. Yes, *please*. But Nome? Who the hell goes to *Nome*?"

Me, that's who.

"I miss him."

"You're a broken record."

"I can't help it."

"You need to get out more," Sil tells me. "Meet new people. Remember how much fun it is here. You only have a few months left at college!"

The thing is? It *isn't* fun here. I'm spoiled for here because Cody isn't here with me.

As I type up the final draft of my study, my memories of the Qimmiq come back in blazing intensity, and I remember that last night on the trail when Cody woke me up to tell me that another team had passed us.

We knew it then. We could both see it. Our chances of planning a future together in the short-term were dashed. Which leaves…what? Nebulous plans of "someday"? How do we hold on to what we have, waiting for an *un*promised "someday" that may never happen?

I read once that friends come into your life for a reason, a season or a lifetime…what if the same is true of romantic relationships? What if Cody and I were only supposed to last for a season—because we were thrown together for a precious few months, and propinquity turned our hearts to each other? When you are apart from the one you love, these sorts of dark thoughts prey on you, and it's so exhausting— the fight *not* to give into them—that sometimes you end up surrendering not from a lack of love, but from a lack of strength.

Be strong, Juliet.

I tell myself that after I graduate, Cody and I can find our way, whatever that is. I tell myself that ours was the love of a lifetime. I tell myself to hold on.

Hold on, Juliet.

I pour myself into my work, writing a fifteen-thousand-word account of my time in Nome, my experiences with the dogs, and my impressions—as a veterinary professional—about sled dog racing, in general. It's the one bright spot of my life since returning to Minnesota: that the fruits of this fellowship are ripe and sweet. My study is good. Empirically good. I'm certain of it.

Rushing to my next-to-last session with Dr. Grant and excited to share my final draft of the study, I slip on the newly waxed floor of the Veterinary Medical Center and fall. My laptop bag, which wasn't securely closed, slides down the hallway like a hockey puck on ice, and my printed paper, moments ago in painstaking chronological order, flies about the corridor in haphazard chaos.

A perfect visual analogy for my life right now: *Everything is a mess since I returned from Nome.*

Two students walking down the hall from the other direction rush to help me gather everything together.

"Thank you," I say, shoving the laptop back in my bag and taking the messy collection of papers from them.

"Your knee is bleeding," points out one of the students.

"Oooo." Her friend cringes. "Better clean that."

"I will," I say, mustering a small smile. "Thanks again."

Limping to Dr. Grant's office, I knock on the door with my elbow. When she opens the door, I don't look up immediately. I rush into the office and plop down on the nearest couch with my handful of papers.

"I'm sorry I'm late," I say. "I dropped my laptop and my notes went everywhere and—"

"Juliet," she says.

I look up to find Professor Steinbuck standing beside her, the shadow of a smirk on his face as he takes in my flustered appearance. Unintentionally, I find myself flick a glance at his nose, which looks fine a month after Cody broke it. My heart clenches at the thought of Cody, although I do feel a small burst of satisfaction remembering the incident.

"What's going on?" I ask.

"I'm going on medical leave." Dr. Grant lowers her hands to her abdomen. "I had pre-eclampsia during my first pregnancy and have decided to take it easy during this one."

"Oh," I murmur, my eyes resting on her flat stomach for a second. "Congratulations. I didn't know you were expecting."

"In my absence, Glenn will be taking over my students as faculty advisor." She holds up her hands, anticipating pushback from me. "I know you two have history, but Glenn's insisting you can work it out. I'd hate for you to have to start over with a *third* faculty advisor this year. Especially so close to the end of your study."

"I'm sorry," I say, glancing at Glenn for a second before shifting my eyes back to Dr. Grant, "but I would, actually, prefer someone else."

"Juliet," Glenn says, "things got blown out of

proportion. Let's just finish up the year, huh?"

I ignore him, focusing on Dr. Grant. "I don't know if you know this, but my boyfriend broke Professor Steinbuck's nose last month. I *really* don't think it's appropriate for us to work together."

"Glenn broke his nose skiing," says Dr. Grant, looking back and forth between us.

"Is that what you told everyone?" I ask, skewering Stein*fuck* with a glare.

And what a smooth liar he is: "Of course that's what I told everyone, Juliet. The truth."

"The truth?" I say, my eyes popping out of my skull. "The truth is that you were my advisor for exactly five days before we started sleeping together, which continued for three weeks before I realized we weren't in an exclusive relationship. I left Minnesota for Alaska asking for a faculty advisor change, which I got. But that wasn't enough for you. You tried to meddle in my project *unsuccessfully*, tracked me down in Alaska, insulted my boyfriend at his home, got your nose broken—which I, for one, think you deserved—and now this? Why, Glenn? Why can't you leave me alone?"

Dr. Grant clears her throat, looking back and forth between us. "I didn't realize…um. My goodness. Glenn?"

He shakes his head. "Seriously, Sheila. She's overdramatizing everything like I told you she would."

"So…you didn't sleep with her?"

"We're both over eighteen and it was consensual."

"But not very ethical," points out Dr. Grant. "I know you went to Alaska. I covered your advisees while you were gone."

"I was there for an Iditarod meeting in Anchorage," says Glenn, "and went skiing with some of the other vets up there for the meeting."

"So you didn't see Miss Sanderson?"

"It doesn't matter," says Glenn.

"I think it does," says Dr. Grant. "Please answer the question."

"I'm not going to dignify it with a response. This was a mistake," says Glenn, looking at me, his eyes furious. "I thought I could take the high road and help you complete your fellowship project—"

"Oh, my God!" I blurt out. "That's it."

"What's *it*?"

"It was never about *me*," I say, staring at Glenn in a new light. "That's what I got wrong all along. It was about my study, wasn't it? You wanted…*what did you want*?" I ask, narrowing my eyes as I think. Then it comes to me. "Oh, my God! I bet you wanted a cowriting credit!"

His face instantly reddens. "What? No. I don't need credit on some undergrad paper. I'm a respected—"

I grin at him because he's so transparent now. "You wanted a cowriting credit on my paper so that you could claim to be an expert in the field of sled dogs and racing. But you didn't want to do the work and research. You just wanted a ride on my coattails."

"That's ridicu—"

"Ridiculous? No, it isn't. You wanted to attach your name to my research and claim it for your own."

"Fuck you, Juliet."

"Glenn!" cries Dr. Grant. "Leave my office immediately! I'll be reporting this incident to the university oversight committee. Expect an investigation into your conduct...*soon*."

Glenn gives me a scathing look before crossing the office to leave, but he pauses at the door, looking at me over his shoulder. "You were a shitty fuck."

"Your nose looks great," I snark as he ducks out the door.

I turn back to Dr. Grant, who rushes to apologize. "I'm *so* sorry about this, Juliet. I had no idea."

"Don't worry," I say. "I don't think he'll be bothering me again."

"I'll make sure of it." She finally realizes my printed study is a disaster. "What happened?"

"I slipped in the hallway."

"Well, let's get it all back in order," she says. "I'll take it with me and read through the final version. I'll also stay on as your advisor to see you through the publication of your study, Juliet. Even if I have to do it from home."

"Thanks, Dr. Grant," I say.

"If my suspicions are right, it'll be good enough for any major veterinary journal, and many more mainstream publications, as well."

"I'm really happy you think so," I tell her, feeling a true burst of pride and happiness in my work.

"And when it's published," she says, "there'll only be one name listed as researcher and author: *yours*."

***

Valentine's Day.

Ugh.

If there's anything more depressing than being twenty-five hundred miles away from the man you love on the year's most romantic day, I don't know what it is.

With my study submitted to four veterinary journals and six other respected news outlets, Dr. Grant assures me that we should be receiving some good news any day. She even believes someone might be willing to pay me for my account of training for a major sled dog race. It's exciting. The only major excitement on my horizon.

I called Cody tonight to thank him for the dozen red roses he sent me, but after two weeks of not speaking at all, it took a few minutes to find our footing, and I think that depressed me more than anything. We're already losing a certain amount of intimacy, which scares me.

Viola is still alive, though Cody thinks the end is near. He falls asleep on the floor beside her most nights, watching her sleep, looking for signs that it's time to call Jonas to come and put her down, but she's still eating a little, and until she gives up on food, he won't make the call.

"Keep me updated about her," I tell him.

"I will," he says, sorrow heavy in his voice.

We talk a little more—about his daily training schedule and how I'm looking forward to moving home—but everything feels strained, like there's so much missing, or lost, between us. It doubles my grief about our separation and fears for our future.

"I love you, Juliet," Cody says toward the end of our conversation. "I think about you every day. All the time."

"Me too," I say. "I love you, too."

"But, God, this sucks, Juliet. It's...so awful. Being apart."

"I know," I say, sniffling as I try to choke back tears.

"I'll try to come visit you in the spring," he says. "Once you're back in Montana working at your dad's practice."

"I'd love that," I say, but he's still talking about two or three months from now, which feels like forever. "I miss you."

"I miss you too," he says before hanging up.

I hug my pillow and cry, which is how Silvia finds me.

"Enough is enough!" she declares. "You're coming out with me tonight."

"On a date? No way!"

"I don't *have* a date," Sil says. "To have a date, I'd need a boyfriend, which I don't. What I *do* have is an invitation to the single's event of the year."

"I'm not single," I say.

She gives me a look which says different, but before I can protest, she says, "Whatever. It's a VD party."

"Sil," I moan, "the *last* thing I want to do is go to a Valentine's Day party!"

"No," she says. "It's not a Valentine's Day party, it's a Venereal Disease party. You dress like your favorite disease in celebration of all the people who are getting infected today. I'm going as the clap. You can be herpes."

"I don't want to be herpes!"

"Chlamydia?"

"No!"

"Just dress up in all red. We'll say you're a tumor."

A testament to my current state of mind is that I actually end up dressed in a red skirt, red T-shirt, and red lipstick, and when people ask, I say I'm a fucking tumor.

"Clever," says a guy by the punchbowl dressed in regular clothes.

"Says the guys who decided not to dress up."

He lifts his shirt a little higher than necessary to showcase cut abs and a preppy belt with needlepoint crabs. Crabs.

"Okay," I say, chuckling. "I get it."

"You know what *I* don't get?" he asks me with a flirty smile.

"What?"

"How you're single. What are you doing here? Why aren't you out celebrating with a significant other?"

"Because my significant other lives in Alaska."

"Long-distance relationship, huh?"

I nod. "Yeah. Something like that."

"Open, by any chance?"

"What do you mean?"

"Is your relationship open? Can you date other people while you're apart?"

"No," I say quickly. "I don't—I mean, no. I'm with him. I love him."

He grins. "Can't blame a crab for trying. Not every day I come across a tumor as cute as you."

I roll my eyes. "Thanks…I guess."

He winks at me before disappearing into the crowd.

A second later, Silvia appears by my side.

"What the heck just happened?" she demands. "Huh?"

"That total hottie just hit on you!"

I shrug. "I'm taken."

"You need a reality check," she announces, taking my elbow and pulling me through the kitchen and outside, onto a back deck. "Your so-called boyfriend is thousands of miles away. You have no plan to see him again—"

"He said he'd visit in April—"

"—no plan for the future. You've been a wreck since you returned. Sincerely, I'm scared for your mental health. You cry all the time. You moon around. You've lost weight. If you're not working or studying, you're miserable. This is crazy, Juliet. You need to snap out of it!"

"How?" I yell. "*How* do I stop loving him? Tell me, Sil, how to make that happen!"

"Let him go for now! And—and if he's the one, you'll find him again…somewhere down the road of life. You'll reconnect when you're ready. But this? Living like this day in and day out? It sucks, Juliet. It's painful to watch!"

"Painful for *you?* Jesus, Sil, *be* more self-centered! You think I *choose* to live like this? You think I *want* to feel like a part of me is missing? You think I *like* crying myself to sleep, living in this—this terrible fucking limbo where the person I want to be with is so far away from me I can't—I can't bear it…Fuck this." I shake my head, blinking back more useless fucking tears. "I'm going home."

"Juliet, wait! Come on. Don't go. I'm sorry."

"Don't worry about it." I shove my red Solo cup at her and stomp down the porch steps. "Have fun."

"I shouldn't have yelled at you! I was trying out some tough love…"

Her voice fades the farther away I get, until I'm halfway home and wondering if there isn't some logic in her awful advice. Maybe we break up for now, live our lives, and then—when and if the time is ever right—we will find each other again.

***

Cody

Viola dies on Valentine's Day.

After I hang up with Juliet, I go outside and feed my dogs, and when I return I can tell. I just…know.

Lying on the bed that Juliet made for her, my Viola is still. Her chest doesn't bob up and down with her breathing. Her eyes don't open to see me. Her tail doesn't wag to greet me. She slipped away while I was outside. She's gone.

I kneel down beside her, wailing with the full measure of my grief: not just for losing Viola, who was the loyalist friend I've ever known, but because I feel so goddamned alone, it's viscerally painful.

My father wouldn't acknowledge me.

My mother didn't love me.

My sister wasn't interested in a relationship with me.

When I lost my hands, I lost my friends, either because

I alienated them, or they were uncomfortable at being whole in the face of my brokenness.

And then there was Vi. She came along and saved my life. She loved me. She saw a me I'd barely dared to hope existed. And from her love, came more dogs. And because of those dogs, eventually, came Juliet.

Now I've lost them both.

Viola is gone forever.

And Juliet is far, far away.

I lie down beside her still-warm body and sob, wishing my girlfriend was here, spooning me from behind, anchoring me to her life the way I once anchored her to mine. I don't wish her to miss out on graduation or anything like that. I know how much she loves being a vet; I would never take that away from her.

I just…fuck, I just miss her so much it hurts.

It's been a month since she left, and I keep waiting for it to get better or easier—to assimilate her absence into my daily life, still knowing that she's out there somewhere loving me, but as time trudges on, it's harder and harder. I keep her shampoo in the shower and use it once in a while, closing my eyes and breathing deeply the smell of her hair. I go upstairs and sit at her desk, looking out on the kennel of dogs she so loved. I visit with Jonas and Rita, who are worried about me; I can see it in their eyes.

Everything is wrong.

Nothing is right.

Apparently, I'm not a man who can love deeply and live apart from his woman. Some men can, I know. I'm not one of them.

Because it's after midnight in Minneapolis and I don't want to risk waking up Juliet with a phone call, I decide to email her to tell her about Vi's passing. She was expecting it. It won't be a shock.

Waiting for me in my in-box, however, is an email from her.

Glancing at the time stamp, I realize she sent it about an hour ago, and it piques my interest. I click on it with anticipation, but what I read knocks the wind out of me.

As if today wasn't already bad enough.

Cody,

I'm staring at the screen, hoping the right words will come to me, but I can't think of any "right" words for what I need to say.

Let me start with what's important: I love you.

I know now that I was never in love before I fell in love with you. I didn't know how love felt—how it bound one life to another in more ways than I could have possibly guessed. I didn't know that being apart from the person I love would be this painful.

I miss you so much, it aches all the time. I cry and I can't sleep, which leads to headaches and trouble concentrating. I've lost weight and I'm sad all the time. I'm making myself sick. I'm driving my roommate crazy. I'm starting to worry about myself.

I've heard about love sickness. Lately, I've been

reading about it too. We're born with the chemicals that make falling in love wonderful. We're also born with the chemicals that make being apart unbearable. We're genetically coded to want to be with our mate. I want to be with you.

And I know we can't be together right now. We both have things to do in different places. It's just that…maybe, if you weren't my mate anymore, my longing would gradually subside to a place where I could bear it.

Tonight, Silvia suggested we break up for a while. She said that if our love is real—which I fervently believe it is—we will find each other again down the road of life. Maybe, if we're not hanging on so tightly, being apart from one another will be more bearable. I don't know how. I just know that we have to do something, because the way we're living now isn't healthy.

I love you, Cody.

Juliet

I read her email once, then twice, then a third time.

Then I pick up Viola gently, take her out to the truck and drive to Jonas's house.

***

"Cody," says Jonas, opening the front door of his house. "Everything okay?"

"Viola passed," I tell him.

"Oh," he says, putting an arm around my shoulder. "Come on in, son. Come sit down."

"Cody! I was just putting on some decaf—" Rita comes bustling out of the kitchen in her bathrobe. "Oh, no. Vi?"

I nod. "She passed in her sleep tonight."

"I'm sorry, Cody. She was a good dog. You brung her here?"

"She's in the truck."

"We'll take her to my office before you go," says Jonas.

There's a crematorium at the highway department that Jonas is allowed to use for pets. I'll scatter Viola's ashes around my property, where she loved to run when she was younger.

"Let me get us some coffee," says Rita, heading back to the kitchen as Jonas and I take a seat across from each other in the TV room.

There's a game show on—the host is asking a contestant about Lady Gaga's songs, and it feels utterly surreal that life is going on as normal everywhere else in the world when mine is, literally, falling apart.

My dog is dead.

And my girlfriend—whom I love more than anyone else in the world—is wondering if we should break up.

"Tough blow to lose a good dog," says Jonas, picking up the remote and turning off the TV. "I know you'll miss her."

I nod, because he's right. I will.

"Juliet emailed me tonight."

"Oh, yeah? How's she doing, then?"

"Not good," I say.

Rita returns with a tray holding three coffee mugs,

cream, sugar, and Oreos. I take the coffee gratefully, but I have no appetite for food. Like Juliet, I've lost weight since we parted. I'm never hungry, even when I train for hours, and absolutely, positively should be.

Lovesick. Yeah. That sounds about right.

"Did I hear you say that Juliet's not doin' good?"

"We miss each other."

Rita nods. "Eat some Oreos."

I ignore the cookies and keep talking. "She wonders if we should break up for a while. You know, take a break. Find each other again down the road."

"Oh, yeah?" asks Jonas, his eyebrows furrowing. "Why's that?"

"Hurts too much to be apart."

"Mmm," hums Rita, stuffing a cookie in her mouth. "'Cause you're training for the Iditarod and she's in school."

"Yeah," I say, taking a sip of coffee. It's hot and strong and I burn my tongue. "I have money saved for the race."

"That's good. Ain't cheap to run a big race like that," Rita observes.

"Ten thousand dollars. It'll get me and my dogs to Anchorage. Lodging. Spruce up my sled. Drop bags. All of it. I can afford it."

Jonas nods. "We'll be waiting for you at the finish line, son."

"If I...If I didn't race," I say, "I could use that ten thousand to fly to Anchorage, buy a dog box, a cheap truck, and drive to Montana."

Jonas stares at me. Rita freezes with a second Oreo

halfway to her lips. I feel like I catch her lips twitch in the glimmer of a smile, but I'm not certain.

"Oh, yeah?" asks Jonas. "Didn't know you were considering a move."

"I'm not," I say. "I mean, I wasn't, but now…I mean, I wouldn't move to Montana forever. Just for the spring and summer. I'd come back in the fall to start training again."

"Sorta split your time between her place and yours, eh?" asks Rita.

I shrug. "I'd miss the Iditarod this year."

"True," says Jonas. "But you'd get the girl."

I look up at him, wishing he was my father, grateful that even though he isn't, he and his wife are my friends, willing to guide and council me.

"What would you do? If you were me?"

"I can't answer that," says Jonas, taking Rita's hand. "I can only tell you what I did." He looks over at his wife, who grins at him with a knowing nod, and continues. "I met Rita thirty years ago in the 1980s. Up here for a few months looking for gold. Racism between whites and natives was worse then than it is now. Her parents weren't thrilled when we fell in love, but mine threatened to disown me—said if I married an 'injun,' I'd be dead to them." His eyes skate to Rita again, and she winks at him. "It occurred to me to let her go—I'm ashamed to say now—because man, it was scary to take that leap, to know that I'd be all alone in the world except for her. But in the end, I knew that nothing could be good if I didn't have her standing next to me. I'd rather have the rest of my life to work out the rest, than have the rest of my life without her."

"And what a bargain he got!" crows Rita, squeezing his hand with a good-natured chuckle. "He got Mitchy. He got a run-down old bar in Nome, Alaska. He got me."

"I got you, babe," Jonas says, grinning at his wife for a long, intimate moment before looking back at me. "Here's what I'm trying to say: Maybe Juliet isn't the thing you need to find down the road. Maybe everything else is."

I stare at Jonas in wonder as something inside of me rejoices, explodes, *comes-to-Jesus*, because the words he's just arranged for me, are the exact words I needed so desperately to hear.

"I could do the Iditarod *next* year," I whisper.

"Or the year after that," says Rita, offering me the whole plate of cookies, which I take on my lap and start eating.

"Or never," I say, stuffing another cookie in my mouth.

"Oh, you should do it," says Jonas. "It's a good dream. But it doesn't have a time limit, son. Just because you decided it was your reason for living don't mean it can't be shoved to the side when a better reason come along."

"Would you watch my place?" I ask. "From March to September? Just stop by once or twice a week and make sure no one's messing with it?"

"You bet I would," says Jonas with a grin, leaning forward to take a cookie before they're all gone.

EPILOGUE #1

Six weeks later

Juliet

I've attended Race for the Sky every year since I was a little girl, but nothing compares to the excitement before the Iditarod, and I am here in Anchorage, on the first Saturday in March, to see it and feel it.

Fourth Avenue is mobbed, four people deep behind barriers. Sponsors are making speeches, but honestly, you can barely hear what they're saying over the whining, howling, and yapping of the teams. The dogs are ready to go, and their energy is contagious.

Quit talking! We want to run!

Suddenly, I focus my attention on the booming voice of the emcee, who starts counting down the start, "Five…four…three…two…ONE!"

My eyes track to the left, and I see the first of seventy-three teams competing shoot down Fourth Avenue, dogs wagging their tails, their red booties a blur as they fly by.

I turn slightly to look over my shoulder at Cody, who's standing behind me.

"You okay?" I ask.

He puts his arms around me and draws me back against

his body. Lowering his head, he whispers by my ear. "I'm great."

"Wish you were out there too?"

"My day will come."

When he called me with his plan: to use the money he was planning to spend on entering the Iditarod to fly himself and his dogs to Anchorage, buy a truck and dog box, and then make the six-day drive to Missoula to stay with me for the spring and summer, my heart burst with happiness.

I quickly came to my senses, however, and told him not to.

While the idea of spending the next six months with him in Montana was heaven, I told him I couldn't bear being the reason that he was putting his Iditarod dreams on hold.

His answer to that?

"*You're* my dream, Juliet. You're the only dream that matters. If all the rest came true, and I didn't have you, none of it would mean a thing."

"But the Iditarod…"

"I'd rather put *it* on hold than *you*. I'll race it next year. Or the year after. Or the year after that. It'll still be there. I've got the rest of my life to enter it, and if you're waiting for me at the finish line, darlin', I'll win it someday. I promise."

We watch five or six more teams, including Jacques Favreau, head out of the chute and run down the road toward Wasilla, wishing every dog and musher the kind of mostly good luck we had in the Qimmiq. Unfortunately, we can't stay the three hours it'll take to watch *all* the teams get started. We have a long drive ahead and eighteen dogs are waiting on us to get going.

The truck and mobile kennel are parked in a garage on Sixth Avenue, and we walk back toward it, hand in hand, through Town Square Park.

"Think I'll like summer in Montana?" asks Cody as we stroll through the snow-covered paths.

"I hope so," I say. "Honestly, I don't think Montana is so different from Alaska in basics. Both have great hiking, fishing, camping. But there's more to see in Montana, more places to go. The road doesn't end after fifty miles. You can drive wherever you want."

"Think the dogs'll like it?"

"The dogs will be happy wherever you are," I tell him, letting go of his hand to walk up some snowy stairs.

"And I'll be happy wherever you are," he says from behind me. "But your mom and dad…"

He's not beside me anymore, so I turn to find him at the foot of the stairs, kneeling in the snow, a small velvet box perched in the palm of his gloved right hand.

"Cody!" I say, stepping down to stand right in front of him. "What are—Oh, my God, are you—"

"Proposing? Yes, I am, darlin', for a couple of reasons," he says. "Two big ones, in fact."

I suck in a deep breath and hold it as I wait for him to continue.

"First, but not foremost: I like your family, Juliet. A lot. So much, in fact, that I am excited to be their son-in-law one day soon. And I just don't think your mom and dad are going to feel comfortable with us shacking up at the cabin unless *promises have been made*," he says, using the same words my mom used in the upstairs hallway at Christmastime when she separated us into different bedrooms.

I giggle through tears, watching as he stands up and opens the box to reveal a beautiful diamond ring.

"Second, and more important than anything else in the world: I love you so much, Juliet—so much more than I ever dreamed I could love another human being. You're my best friend, my partner, my teammate, and my lover. If I'm not with you, what's the point of anything? Honestly, what's the point of a life if the person you love most in the world isn't a part of it? So I promise you right now that not distance, nor injury, nor weather, nor money, nor... anything else, will keep us apart. Not ever. Not if I have anything to say about it. The only life I want is the one I spend with you." He blinks his eyes furiously. "Juliet, darlin'...will you marry me?"

"Yes!" I manage to whisper through tears, tearing off my glove and placing the beautiful ring on the fourth finger of my left hand.

It sparkles in the bright sun, and a feeling of so much tenderness, so much gratitude overwhelms me, making my knees weak. So I throw my arms around him, knocking him off-balance, and we fall backward into the snow, laughing and kissing as folks coming and going to the Iditarod pause in surprise to see a young couple making out in the snow.

We're red-cheeked and snowy when we finally stand up.

"She's going to marry me," Cody murmurs, clasping my

cheeks with his gloved hands and kissing me again.

"The sooner the better," I say, putting my gloves back on, careful not to snag the diamond setting. "I love you."

"I love you, too," he says, leading me back onto the path that leads to the parking garage.

We open the dog box for a second, just to say hello to the dogs and tell them our news before we get started. We'll stop halfway in Glenallen for a pee and run break, and finish our drive in Tok, Alaska. I found a bed-and-breakfast where the owner didn't mind having eighteen dogs running around her backyard for an evening.

As I sit down in the cab next to Cody, he leans over and kisses me tenderly.

"You ready for this, Juliet?"

I kiss him back. "With you? My Nome-o? I'm ready for anything."

He turns the key and off we go, ready for the adventure of a lifetime, and a lifetime of adventures…together.

EPILOGUE #2

Three Years Later

DAILY NEWS

World · Buisness · Finance · Lifestyle · Travel · Sport · Weather

March 19, 2023   Anchorage's longest-running publication   № 767417720з

NEW MUSHER WINS BIG AT IDITAROD!

Anchorage, AK - The biggest upset at the 2023 Iditarod race? Cody M. Garrison, this year's champion, whose team, led by Malamute-mixes, Dover and Boston, trotted across the finish line in Nome at 3:42am, ten minutes earlier than last year's winner, Jacques Favreau. Mr. Favreau, the favorite to win, crossed the finish line fourteen minutes later at 3:56am.

Mr. Garrison, a retired United States Marine Corps veteran, has made recent headlines as one of the first physically-handicapped mushers to reach this level of success in sled dog racing.

As he crossed the finish line, he was cheered on by hundreds of fans, chanting his name, whooping and cheering. Alaskan Native dancers performed, while friends and family congratulated Mr. Garrison and his team. But Mr. Garrison sought only one face in the crowd, and once he found her, he shared a long, emotional embrace with his wife, well-known sled-dog veterinarian, Juliet Sanderson Garrison, and their 2-year-old daughter, Viola.

"My wife and daughter are everything to me," said Mr. Garrison. "I won this race for them."

The Garrisons split their time between Nome, Alaska, and Missoula, Montana, Mrs. Garrison's home town. One can only imagine what this power-couple of sled dog racing has in store, but all of Alaska, *all of the world*, will be watching.

THE END

ALSO BY KATY

a modern fairytale
(A collection)

The Vixen and the Vet
Never Let You Go
Ginger's Heart
Dark Sexy Knight
Don't Speak
Shear Heaven
Fragments of Ash

THE BLUEBERRY LANE SERIES

THE ENGLISH BROTHERS
(Blueberry Lane Books #1–7)

Breaking Up with Barrett
Falling for Fitz
Anyone but Alex
Seduced by Stratton
Wild about Weston
Kiss Me Kate
Marrying Mr. English

THE WINSLOW BROTHERS
(Blueberry Lane Books #8–11)

Bidding on Brooks
Proposing to Preston
Crazy about Cameron
Campaigning for Christopher

THE ROUSSEAUS
(Blueberry Lane Books #12–14)

Jonquils for Jax
Marry Me Mad
J.C. and the Bijoux Jolis

THE STORY SISTERS
(Blueberry Lane Books #15–17)

The Bohemian and the Businessman
The Director and Don Juan
Countdown to Midnight

THE SUMMERHAVEN SERIES

Fighting Irish
Smiling Irish
Loving Irish
Catching Irish

THE ARRANGED DUO

Arrange Me
Arrange Us

ODDS ARE GOOD SERIES

Single in Sitka
Nome-o Seeks Juliet
A Fairbanks Affair
My Valdez Valentine
Kodiak Lumberjack

STAND-ALONE BOOKS:

After We Break
(a stand-alone second-chance romance)

Frosted
(a stand-alone romance novella for mature readers)

Unloved, a love story
(a stand-alone suspenseful romance)

**Under the sweet-romance pen name
Katy Paige**

THE LINDSTROMS

Proxy Bride
Missy's Wish
Sweet Hearts
Choose Me
Virtually Mine
Unforgettable You
My Treasure – all new!
Summer's Winter – all new!

**Under the paranormal pen name
K. P. Kelley**

It's You, Book 1
It's You, Book 2

**Under the YA pen name
Callie Henry**

A Date for Hannah

ABOUT THE AUTHOR

New York Times and *USA Today* bestselling author **Katy Regnery** started her writing career by enrolling in a short story class in January 2012. One year later, she signed her first contract, and Katy's first novel was published in September 2013.

More than forty books and three RITA® nominations later, Katy claims authorship of the multititled Blueberry Lane series, the A Modern Fairytale collection, the Summerhaven series, the Arranged duo, and several other stand-alone romances, including the critically acclaimed mainstream fiction novel *Unloved, a love story*.

Katy's books are available in English, French, German, Hebrew, Italian, Polish, Portuguese, and Turkish.

Made in the USA
Lexington, KY
08 November 2019

56730102R00151